Not Quite Duppy

A Collection Of Short Stories For Jamaican Readers

Sez Hoo

MOONSHINE ON BIG YARD ROAD

In Jamaica people are superstitious. Sometimes superstitions totally guide their daily activities; what they dare to do and what they dare not try. In many situations the fears that are built up are just fears but in other instances they become a little more and remain questionable. In Jamaica there is the practice of Obeah as well and people pay big money to people who live in remote, desolate places, to have them invoke curses and charms on other individuals. As an onlooker it is easy to conclude that the person being cursed is deserving of it, but does the charms and invoked curses actually work, and are those supposedly stricken individuals always guilty?

Warsop in southern Trelawny is a place populated by people steeped in traditional African beliefs and the practice of Obeah to settle differences and to get revenge on those who have wronged them. Rural Saint Catherine is another such place. One only need to think of places like Point Hill, Water Mount, Kentish and such districts to get the creepy feeling that more spirits reside in them than humans. Kingston on the other hand, the big city was too well lit for Duppies, Rolling Calves, Three-Foot Jacks, Whooping Boys and the like to reside, or for Obeah men to practise their necromancy.

I am Sam, and I was born in the Victoria Jubilee Hospital in Western Kingston, *"unda di clock"* as the saying goes. My family moved to rural Jamaica in 1972 amidst severe rioting across the Jones Town and Trench Town communities of western Kingston. I was not almost seven years old at the time of our hasty departure. We settled in a district known as Warsop, somewhere in the mountainous region of southern Trelawny. I remained there with my family until I graduated High School. I was by then all of seventeen years. Having lived in

Warsop for ten years I learnt quite a bit about the culture of the place and have seen quite a bit manifested right in front of me from the realm of the spirits and so on.

I shared this story with a friend of mine one day as we sat under his favourite tree, and I am now sharing it with you:

One night while I was still a student at Holmwood Technical High School, I arrived home in Warsop rather late. This was not uncommon since Holmwood was situated in the parish of Manchester, some sixteen miles away from my home in Warsop. The challenge facing me was to make it home from the Crossroads where the vehicle I had hopped onto, slowed enough for me to jump off without hurting myself, all the way over to where I lived on a rented property called Big Yard. To get to Big Yard I had to walk out of the brightly lit crossroads onto Baptist road, which went up a fairly steep incline for about 70 meters to where an old stone building stood with its rear wall overlooking a Cemetery and part of the Baptist Church property. The old building was once the place of worship for the Baptists but had been abandoned out of fear of a lack of structural integrity due to its age. There was another streetlight right after the old church building, the gate of the district's only Justice of the Peace; an old lady named Florence Milford and affectionately called Ms. Facey. That night I got as far as the streetlight outside Ms. Facey's gate and stopped, rooted to the spot, overcome by a sinister dread as I stared into the thick darkness that lay ahead of me, starting where the grove of Mango trees hung over the roadway. That night as I stood under the light outside the gate of the Justice of the Peace, peering up slope, I could not see that there was a moon out. I stood there thinking for a long time about how I would be getting home and an icy fear gripped me and kept me rooted there, where the last street lamp, overlooking the Baptist Cemetery on the left side of the road, shared its treasured light with the night. That was little comfort as more than forty gravestones stared blankly at me, as though daring me to venture in. Finally, I decided that I wouldn't venture any place, and definitely not into that pitch-black nothingness ahead. Instead I opted for passing the night on the steps that led up into Ms.

Facey's kitchen. Ms. Facey's house was on the side of the road opposite the Church Cemetery. I quietly made my way down behind the garage at the front where uncle Bam had parked his Austin Cambridge while he was alive, between the unused water Tank, and onto the steps. There I rested my heavy school bag down and made myself as comfortable as I could. There was no one to talk to so being quiet was not a problem for me. Now I wished, and hoped and prayed for morning to come, but I would soon discover how long a night could be. I dozed off a few times and woke each time anticipating dawn, but on each occasion I was disappointed because only a short time had passed. At long last I decided that the night was dragging on just a bit too long and that I would get up, muster up enough courage, and head home. The night had gotten quite chilly by then and the light from the moon was now apparent over the Cemetery. No light broke through the Mango grove along the roadway however and I remember shivering as I stared into the gross darkness again. My mind was made up however to conquer my fear and head home. I just started walking, into the darkness which quickly swallowed me. To my surprise, once inside it was not as dark as when viewed from outside. I felt emboldened and encouraged and I pushed forward. Suddenly I was able to see the crest of the hill ahead of him, and the open sky, and moon light. I was not prepared for what I saw the very next moment. An extremely tall, lanky figure, no less than forty feet tall, dressed in Khaki suit, stepped into view at the top of the hill emerging from the left side of the road. I blurted out the name of the Lord followed by a few Jamaican expletives before my belly muscles knotted up and I find myself unable to breathe properly.

"Mi dead tonight, lawd god, a wha dat mi a si!" I grunted, swallowing a mouthful of saliva and almost choking on it.

One extremely long leg appeared first, and I stopped and stared up in awe, trying to see up to the crotch of that Khaki pant which was so high up in the sky. Then the second leg swung across the ten feet wide roadway, landing in McArthur's yard. I stood frozen to the spot as the hind leg followed, and the figure disappeared into the dark backgrounds as it continued its midnight journey to wherever it was heading. I was extremely shaken up but I did not turn back. Several minutes later, after getting over the brief encounter with the paranormal, and resuming his journey home, I was again walking along the rugged parochial road in the shadows of trees. I passed by Helen Que Que's place, passed Maas Daniel's place, and Ms. Doll's place, and then onto the footpath that was a quarter of a mile long, through a valley. Approximately fifty meters along this narrow footpath I had to contend with another bit of strangeness. Right beside the path there was an Old Isaac tree, maybe as old as its name. I have passed this spot in the night before and had observed a large circular green area midway up its trunk that glowed a bright green, neon type light. I had heard scary rumours about this tree, one of them being that it had been planted to mark the spot of a grave and therefore I inferred that the green light was the manifestation of the ghost of whoever that dead person had been. On this night however I decided, maybe after having seen the tall sky walker, that this eerie tree was no longer that creepy to me, so I stopped and stared at the tree. I have always wondered whether the rumours were true and so I acted on the urge to reach out and touch the light. As I scraped my fingers in the green, I positioned my other palm so that anything falling would be collected, and I immediately felt tiny particles hitting my upturned palm. Then it dawned on me that I was still standing, and breathing, and I sighed in relief. Many tiny green lights were now glowing from the middle of my palm. Time continued its march now after stopping when I decided to venture into the realm of my fear. Closing my fist around whatever those particles were, I resumed my journey home, in the silence that marked the night always, along this footpath. Yes there were the sounds of crickets, and a myriad other night bugs, and backing them up in their chorus was the occasional snapping of a dry twig here or there in the shadows cast by the different trees that hung over the narrow footpath. I was petrified but brave I guess, because I had been told the story of the two duppies that always walked together and about how they would argue over whether I had freedom of passage along this path. Whoever told me, had said that the good duppy would demonstrate to the bad duppy that whoever was passing had the right of passage if they looked around frantically whenever he snapped a dry twig. And so every time I heard the snapping twig my head would swivel in the direction of the sound to see what I would see, but every time I would be disappointed, while the good duppy laughed at the bad one and said, you see, this one is mine and he has the right of passage, leave him alone. After another three nerve wracking minutes of hasty strides and furtive glances, I arrived home at the top of a rise where Big Yard was located. The yard was brightly lit as I strode purposefully across toward the front door. The house was as silent as a classroom during the summer holidays. I shared my encounter with brer Sheelz my father, who after looking me over carefully, said this to me,

"how yu feelin' bway?!" He rested the back of his palm against my neck briefly and checked my temperature. As he did so I slowly opened my clenched fist under the light from the Lamp and stared at my palm. There in the hollow of my hand were several tiny plants, each with an even more tiny green light shining from its centre. It

turned that each green light was being emitted by a miniscule bug that lives in the seedy bark of the Old Isaac tree. I opened the door and dusted my hands on the verandah.

"These things could be used as a light source brer Sheelz, they remind me of the peenie wallie but they only much smaller!" I remarked, relieved that I had discovered the secret to the mysterious, eerie green glow that had for so long held many residents of Warsop believing that a ghost lived at that Old Isaac tree. The twig snapping and the two duppies I would investigate another day but right now I was very satisfied.

"lissen!", brer Sheelz voice brought me out of my reverie, *"yu gwine have to stop comin' home so late from School yu hear mi!"*

"wha' yu see out dey a while ago is a serious thing yu hear mi, dem call dem ol' slave driva, an dem sey if him did crack him whip an it ketch yu yu dead like di puss a Norway!"

"Back when mi use to go a Dance mi did see one a dem dung inna Holland Bamboo aroun' after three one mawnin' when mi was walkin' back home from a Dance". "Dat night when mi see di man a walk a gwaan before mi, mi get happy thinking mi have company fi go home, but all di walk mi a walk up fast mi couldn't ketch up wid di man!"

"Dat was when mi realize how tall di man was an mi sey to mi'self, no wonda mi c'yaa ketch him up!"

As modern Christian people we nuh believe inna dem kinda tings but dem dey out dey, an according to the story tellers them kind inna the khaki suit was maybe one of dem who use to watch over di slave dem inna dis ya region a south Trelawny okay...gwaan go tek off yu clothes an cum eat yu dinner, yu mus' tiad"

I changed my clothes and found my way into the small Dining room where my father had placed a wide plate on which there were three fairly large round dumplings, two fingers of hardboiled green bananas, two pieces of chicken parts and a small mound of Ackee and Salted fish. After approximately six minutes I had made all the food disappeared and was taking my plate into the kitchen. Brer Sheelz had retired to his bed now, having stayed up to make sure that I had made it home safely from School. I washed my mouth and drifted off into my bedroom to join my siblings who were sound asleep.

The End.

Joe's Tenure
A Baptism in mud

By: Sez Hoo

"To diminish a light is to reduce the light that shines from a source by erecting shades and blinds in the spectrum of its rays until its light no longer reaches or brightens anything"- *attributed to the author*

This is a strange story of twelve years in the beautiful island of Grand Bahama as recounted by a Jamaican teacher.

One man's life as it unfolded while he served in the Department of Education; His reflection on his restless life, and an unforgiving system to which he had been exposed; where a small ring of unscrupulous individuals operating within the department of education would stop at nothing to nullify his life. The attending drama and so many other interesting things are the subject of this narrative.

CHAPTER 1

Going UP!

Joe migrated to the Bahamas from Jamaica in 2006. He went there to teach in the Government Education System. He was to spend many years there as his Contract was renewed on three occasions with each Contract lasting three years. Joe was excited primarily because as a teacher in his homeland he was not making enough money to make ends meet as the saying goes. Moving to the Bahamas meant more money in his pocket at the end of the month, and a breather away from the stresses of a third world country languishing in the ebb and flow of a bad economy brought on it as a result of poor decisions made by former leaders of that nation. And so it was that on August 30th, 2006 Joe landed in New Providence, Nassau to take up his position as a teacher in the Bahamas Department of Education.

"Are you Joseph Shelteroch?!" a short, gray haired gentleman smiled at him from behind rimmed glasses as

he sat in the Waiting Area of the Lynden Pindling

International Airport. The older gentleman was holding a

Placard with 'Joseph Shelteroch' type written on it. Joe

smiled, *"Yes sir, that's me, finally!"* as he jumped to his

feet.

"Follow me please!", He stretched out his hand and

shook with Joe, *"let me take you to your destination.*

Welcome to the Bahamas sir, it's my pleasure on behalf

of the Department and Ministry of Education to officially

welcome you to our fair islands. I hope you will enjoy

your stay with us as we endeavour to mould the minds of

tomorrow's leaders and great men"

He followed the small man through a few glass doors

and along an enclosed corridor, and then into a wide

open space where many persons were standing in line

waiting to speak with a man at a Counter. A sign above

the Counter read, 'Bahamas Customs'.

The older gentleman instructed Joe to join the line and

declare to the officer at the Counter who he was and

what his purpose for being in the Bahamas was. Then he

told him he would be back and left him there.

Half an hour or so later Joe got to the front of the line and showed the officer his Passport and a letter that the elderly man had given him. He was processed and asked to sit in another Waiting Area until his chaperone returned. This wait was long, and it seemed much longer to Joe because he was hungry and alone, without currency with which to even purchase food.

The elderly gentleman returned late in the afternoon and Joe was whisked off to the Towne Hotel where he spent two nights before being given a Ticket and placed on a flight to Grand Bahama. At the Towne there were several other Jamaicans waiting to be transferred to the island and School in which they were needed but Joe left them there.

It was a great feeling being outside of Jamaica and he was elated knowing that it wasn't to be a short vacation but a long term arrangement. On arrival in Grand Bahama he was picked up at the Airport by a Caucasian male who introduced himself as Mr. Zedekiah Been, who took him on a brief tour through the city of Freeport to a Best Western Hotel, now popularly known as Castaways Hotel. Mr. Been had already made arrangements with the Hotel for his accommodation and so checking in was a quick process. One swipe card for the room door and access to the Restaurant was given to him when he was directed to where he would be staying along with instructions regarding meal times on the property. All Joe had to do was breathe to enjoy the experience.

"Mr. Been, thank you so much for everything so far sir, I guess we will see each other around sometimes" They shook hands.

"Remember you will be picked up for School on Monday by someone from the school you have been posted so be ready and waiting at 7:15, and that afternoon you need to come and meet with me and other members of a Panel at the Ministry building to finalize a few details regarding your employment status here, bring all your Certificates with you when you are coming on Monday, take good care"

With that the tall lanky man walked away leaving Joe absorbing his new reality as resident on the island. He closed the door and dropped himself on the closest seat to collect his thoughts. It had been a busy day.

The following morning was Saturday and Joe did not know the location of any Seventh Day Adventist Church as yet, so he took the opportunity to explore the island a bit. He set out to see where his place of employment was located. He was told it was in an area known as Eight Mile Rock. A long slow ride on a small Minibus took him through parts of the city and then out onto a long straight stretch of smooth roadway which only changed direction at a Stoplight where there was a sign that read Brewery. From there the road continued, winding a little followed by long straight stretches again until Joe saw a sign through the window indicating that he was entering Eight Mile Rock. A few minutes after the sign the bus stopped and he was pointed along a road which the driver told him leads to the campus. He paid the $.75 and the vehicle drove away. Thirty minutes later he was on his way back to Freeport in another Minibus. Joe had seen enough and was satisfied that he could find his way to and from work if he needed to.

Monday morning came and Joe stood waiting in the Lobby of the Hotel from as early as 7:00 A.M.

Like clockwork a small vehicle rolled up under the arched Portico. A man stepped out dressed in shirt and tie and walked toward him smiling, *"I assume you are Mister Shelteroch!"* he said.

"Yes I am sir, I am expecting to be picked up for work here this morning!"

"I am Mr. Polle and I am that pick up person you are waiting on, please come with me"

At the car they shook hands before entering and driving away.

"So Mister Shelteroch how has it been so far for you, what is this, your fourth day in the island?"

"Yes I came in on Friday afternoon, and it has been great for me so far, the place is beautiful too, thanks for asking" Joe looked across and smiled at his chauffeur, *"I am looking forward to meeting the students and staff this morning!"*

"I am sure you are going to like working here Mr. Shelteroch and I will be part of the team that ensures that your experience is a good one, don't worry your head, you can always come to me when you need

assistance or information at school. I will show you my office when we get there"

It was high energy at school among the students as they relived their long summer break with their friends and showed off their latest electronic acquisition. The teachers were a bit less hyped up because they may have worked throughout the break and were not mentally ready for this return.

The weeks following his arrival went by slowly as he adjusted to life in a new place and outside of Jamaica. Mr. Polle, Senior Master as Joe discovered, picked him up every morning and dropped him off in the afternoons, rain or shine and they enjoyed light pleasant conversations on the journey to and from school as both men shared about their places of birth and living in these places.

"I have noticed how wet and green everything here looks Mister Polle, Joe expressed one morning as they drove along, *"what is the reason or secret for that?!"*

"Oh I should have mentioned it to you, we just passed through a hurricane. You can still see debris piled up in some places right now, over there for example!" Mr. Polle pointed out the window at a pile of tree trunks that had been chain-sawn into approximately six foot lengths and heaped on a lawn along the way. *The island is really still in recovery mode right now"*

"I must admit that I am enjoying it", Joe surprised him, *"it is a most welcome change from the scorching temperatures of Kingston where I am from, praise God for that"*

CHAPTER 2

Life in the Rocks

Working in Eight Mile Rock was a whole new paradigm shift for Joe. He was accustomed to teaching students who were actually interested in learning and examination results. At this new school the students were mostly interested in how nice their uniforms fitted them. Doing well in school work was relegated to those students from Haitian homes among them. Joe discovered how social promotion was the order of the day and particular students after wasting time in his classes saw nothing wrong with approaching him and asking him to adjust their final grade upwards so they may qualify for a Scholarship, or to go out and represent the country or school. There were even teachers who approached Joe to top-up grades for the odd athlete in order for him to qualify to go out with a Sports team.

Being at School seem to be only a daily routine of escaping the rigors of home and gain the valuable experience of s pending the Lunch money, and yes enjoy the opportunity to show off on each other and engage in illicit sexual activities. The girls came ready, and the boys were never to be outdone. Of course in all fairness to the students, not all of them were ever guilty of this poor attitude toward their education. The children of Haitian parents who lived in Haitian homes were always positive, focused and very humble. They needed to be because there were pressures on them at home to do well, and pressure at School to stay at the top in order to be allowed to remain in the system, at least until they turned eighteen. While the average student kept themselves neatly attired most of the time, the Haitian ones stood out among them in that regard. Something else that caught Joe's attention was the practice that girls had of throwing up their skirts anywhere they had a fancy to do so in order to get to their blouse or whatever else they needed to retrieve from under it. They literally did this anywhere. They would just sit right down in the grass where it was possible to be sitting in mucous from somebody's throat, or wet earth which would stain the blue tunic they wore. The boys did this to a lesser extent but often times there were those who would turn up at School wearing dirty, unwashed uniforms on a Monday morning. Other boys wore pants far beyond their retirement date after the blue had totally burnt out in spots, and sad to say, a few of them carried a foul odour with them as they moved, suggesting that they were not taking regular showers at home, and the odour was not always that of unwashed bodies and clothes, there was another really funky odour that suggested that they were engaging in strange sexual behaviours, either willingly or under coercion at home and in their communities. They were poor children, who put on a good show of being wealthy whenever they were out in public and especially in the presence of a foreigner. Lunch time was the best time of the day because break time was too short. The big 8 inch square by 3 inches deep Styrofoam containers filled with rice and Turkey, or Chicken meat, pasta salad baked or otherwise, swimming in gravy, and a soda of their choosing was their staple calorie intake daily, which left them too drowsy to properly concentrate in their classes. This drowsiness was a welcome past time for many of them as they were allowed the pleasure of dropping their heads on desks and dozing off. The flip side to that would be the soda sugar rush which made some of them extremely hyperactive and rightly fitted to be disruptive during lessons. Not much ever got done by way of academics on that campus. The cream of the crop students who defied the odds around them, were really very few.

'Cutting movies' was another highlight of the school day at that school. It was those fleeting moments when two or more irate students sprung into action, at each others' throats to defend their honour in the presence of their peers. It was when clothes got ripped and shoes got lost, and the noise level suddenly shot up to high decibels. It was that time when a class full of partly attentive students would suddenly become empty, leaving the teacher in shock, or rushing out as well to part a fight and maybe save a life. This was superb fun for those fun-loving students. The passage of such a fracas as described would end with the distraught, torn up, crying parties being hauled off to the long bench outside the Principal's office to wait their turn to complain, the end result of which may be a few swipes of a Cane administered in love by either the Dean of discipline or the Principal himself, and that would be over. However, if a Haitian child made that mistake, which they rarely did, it would be a whole different ending for them. Somebody would be suspended or permanently removed from the school. One such episode unfolded in the following way:

FIGHT!!!...FIGHT!!! Somebody had shouted those words from inside a classroom as a girl and a boy got into a tussle near the centre of the room next door. Suddenly there was a loud raucous sound as chairs and desks were hastily pushed back to release the flood of students from the classrooms along the block.

MOVIE!!! They shouted, rushing out the doors to where the two combatants were now locked by their left hands to their chest and bosom while the two right hands were rapidly swinging back and forth, *WHOOSH! WHOOSH! WHOOSH!* followed by *PLAT! PLAT! PLAT!* as they rained blows to the head, face and bodies of each other. The mob of blue and white got to the spot in a flash and quickly sided with the combatant they preferred, turning the two-man event into a brawl straight out of this world. Students from the Sea Grape community rushed to the aid of their friend while those from Jones Town barged

in to help their friend throw blows at the Sea Grape
student. Fists, open palmed slaps, shoes, both toe kicks
and full bottomed stomp downs were being delivered at
high velocity by both of the original combatants. This
vicious attack only became worse as members of both
gangs turned their wrath on each other, so that now it
was several people fighting several people about
something they really knew absolutely nothing about. A
few teachers, followed by the Dean of discipline got
there last but in time to prevent one wild eyed boy from
swinging an old Desk into the enraged, railing, agitated,
blood thirsty crowd. The tall Dean of discipline broke
through to the centre and grabbed a hold of the two who
had started the whole thing and dragged them off to the
Principal's office.

"You boy, come with me as well!" he signalled to the
boy who was about to throw the Desk. Crazy is the word
for the scene.

Apart from the fights there was Jonkanoo preparations
that energized the students. Jonkanoo Parades or 'Rush
out' as it is called locally, happened annually at
Christmas time and during the early days of the New

Year. These parades were the highlight of all Bahamians. It is an awe inspiring scene to take in as revellers in masks and fancy costumes performed coordinated dance moves along designated routes in the city of Freeport. It amazes the onlooker to see how ordinary food barrels are used to produce the awesome bass that reverberates through the evening when a parade is passing. The entire street is taken over and decorated, first by signs and banners and small kiosks for selling goodies, and then by the bouncing, jolly crowd. The Cow Bells, horns, Bass Trumpets, Saxophones, whistles, smaller drums added to any other kind of musical instrument combine to produce a sound that is truly unique and amazing, and the beauty about it is that the parade happens without the need to connect to any electrical source. Then the blaze of colours makes for another high and to top it all off were the beautiful ladies who made the fabric and costumes work at the front of the parade as they showed off their dancing skills. Jonkanoo is a celebration not to be missed when one is in the Bahamas. Yes, and so students anticipate Jonkanoo and often dream of even the preparation which includes the actual designing and making of the costumes which are usually from everyday materials available in food stores or out in the open natural environment. It is simply mind boggling what the people are able to create out of the items they collect. One has to witness the elaborate floats that depict the theme to believe that it's actually possible.

Regarding the teachers, they were always, most of them, looking for opportunities to dodge their work, and would as a result merely babysit the restless, overfed, undernourished children until whenever the bell went for ending a lesson. They could put on a good show though, when it became time for the officers from the Ministry to conduct Evaluation: those classroom walls would be made so pretty with Charts purchased at Bellevue or imported from Florida that the conclusions about their performance as teachers would often be inaccurate. Teachers have even taken bribes in the form of goodies for the students on Evaluation day in an effort to keep them quiet. The foreign teachers would not fare that well under scrutiny. They had to have proper work in place; lesson plans, unit plan, effective classroom management techniques and a pleasant countenance in order to score well on that ACR.

The Gym for Assemblies, the Staffroom for the frequent Staff meetings, the annual Sports Day at the Sports Complex in Freeport, Island Sports and games competitions locally and in Nassau, the annual meetings in one of the island's school Gym where all teachers met for recharging, soon became the norm for Joe as the nine years and three Contracts spent themselves. He dreamt of moving back home and purposed in his heart that he would do so in the year that he turned fifty. He often had day dreams about Jamaica; the roadways, the lush landscapes, the mountains, the cool breeze available even when the sun was out in all its glory, the people, the language, and so many other interesting things. It just wasn't the same in the Bahamas for him.

During those years, as he learnt the ways and culture of the Eight Mile Rock School and its constituents, a few interesting things happened in Joe's life which made it challenging for him to keep a smile on his face even with his best effort.

The first incident had to do with his wife that he had sent for shortly after migrating into the employ of the Bahamas Government. This started off with his wife suspecting him of having an affair with another female on the island. Her jealousy would not allow her to rest eyes or limbs and so Joe could not rest either from her gaze and constant monitoring. This episode unfolded at the High School where he had been placed there to teach Technical subjects and to be Homeroom teacher for a group of senior students. In his first year those students were big and quite adult in their conduct on campus. Although Joe was a married man he found himself staring at a particular student more than he should. She was obviously the oldest in his Homeroom and she was of Haitian descent. Joe had nothing but love for Haitians, maybe because he observed how they were mistreated by the Bahamians and the fact that he knew their history as a people and how strong and formidable they really were in the defence and preservation of their nation before sanctions were placed on them by the British Monarchy. Him being a foreigner he naturally sided with this group although he scarcely ever expressed his feelings to anyone. The jealousy of his insecure wife actually led Joe to consider following through with secret desires he had for this Haitian girl. Things however did not work out because the student had to discontinue her schooling prematurely upon turning eighteen. Joe really had strong feelings for Girlie and he had whispered as much to her on one occasion when he got the chance to speak with her alone. Making headway was difficult though because Girlie spoke very little English. In the end Joe only got to buy her a Scientific Calculator as a gift. To make a long story short, the Immigration Task Force, responsible for picking up illegal immigrants came to the School one day but a group of them, including Girlie, narrowly escaped, assisted of course by Joe who squeezed them into his car and left the Campus just moments before the dark blue Minibus arrived. With his dream of Girlie fading, Joe had to settle for the otherwise interesting life that Eight Mile Rock presented to him: bush fires and mouldy buildings, plumbing that didn't work properly, and a big Gym with an Air-conditioning system that often failed, as Principals came and went, five times in total, became part and parcel of the lot he had drawn.

At the same time however, Joe had become very unhappy with his wife. She had become dissatisfied with his money management abilities and would sometimes make him feel small by paying for the goods in the Food Store while he was standing right there, a definite slap in the face for many men of African descent. Additionally it is a fact that Jamaican women when given the opportunity to choose a spouse while living outside of Jamaica, will choose a male of a different nationality over a Jamaican male. It was what it was, and so Joe's wife, as he was to find out much later, had begun making plans to divorce him for an older British citizen she had been introduced to by one of her Jamaican girlfriend who she kept in touch with. Her plan unravelled in the following way: Joe had travelled to Jamaica one summer holiday, leaving her and her daughter at home in Freeport. While in Jamaica he learnt that her grown son had thrown a stone and broken a street lamp, for which he was expected to appear in Court to face charges. As husband he called and informed his wife of what the things he had heard, inclusive of characters that her son was hanging out with. To his surprise she boarded a flight and turned up in the country to conduct her own investigation. She found the individuals and subsequently befriended them, as well as assisting her son with his Court charge. Joe was hurt by her befriending the folks and making him out to be someone who just loved picking on her son because he didn't like the young man and so the relationship was tense, resulting in them returning to the Bahamas on separate flights. Back in Freeport they remained aloof and argued frequently about the situation her son had gotten himself into. Before the end of the Christmas term she had had enough and she started spreading rumours about her husband around the island, mostly to teachers and members of the local Church they attended. She told stories of physical, psychological, mental and sexual abuse to the itchy ears she encountered until her conduct and the supposed behaviour of her husband reached the ears of the District Superintendent. She also moved out of the apartment without his knowledge and went to stay with a colleague. The District Superintendent had her transferred to another School immediately. Joe remained in that apartment until the end of the Christmas term. During that time he sought out a cheaper apartment and moved out in December with his small daughter and kept her with him for a few weeks before taking her back to her mother in Jamaica.

The New Year came and his wife continued her subtlety by seeking and finding out where he was now living. Knowing her, she was either horny or had something sinister up her sleeve. By the end of February she had tracked him down and begun her pleading for him to return to her. Joe, being aware of the ills of being alone, gave in to her request and moved in with her around Easter of that year. Big mistake!.

He moved in to her apartment in April and sure, he did live there without incident until the summer break came. Then he went home as his custom was and stayed until late August. When he returned there was a surprise waiting for him. First his wife introduced him to friends she had staying in the apartment with her. There were two older white men and two females who spoke Jamaican Patois fluently. Joe greeted them as they moved their belongings out and he dismissed the whole thing almost immediately. It was understandable: he had left her alone with his small daughter and her daughter for the summer and she had brought a few friends in to spend time with her, no big deal. After all hadn't he enjoyed himself in Jamaica?

He never saw those people again but after a few weeks thoughts came together in his head, urging him to answer the question, "who were these people he had awkwardly met inside his wife's apartment, and he dedicated himself to finding the answer to it.

The answer came to him a few weeks into the new school year. That summer his wife had invited visitors, one of them her lover, into the apartment and they had spent the time together. The male visitors were British and they were accompanied by two females from Jamaica. It turned out that his wife had been introduced to one of the gentlemen by one of her Jamaican girlfriends. The men were father and son, both of them older men. Her friend introduced her to the father and kept the son for herself. The sister of her friend had just come along to the Bahamas for the ride and used her time to fraternize with the Bahamian male population.

One afternoon, out of the blue, Joe's wife approached him, as he returned home from work: *"Do you remember telling me that I need to know when I have had enough of something?!"*

He did not understand the significance of the question at that time. He knew he had done nothing unusual or wrong to her, so he was surprised by the question and waited to see where she was heading with the conversation.

He nodded and she continued, *"well I have had enough of this, of us together, so I am asking you right now to pack your things and leave my apartment, thank you!"* she stared up into his face, eyes unblinking as she spoke.

He was calm, *"You mean like right this minute, today, this evening?!"*

"Yes Joseph Shelteroch, this evening!", she shouted, frowning at him.

"At least let me stay tonight and try to arrange for somewhere to move to in the morning, okay"

"No!" she insisted, raising her voice, *"if you let night catch you here I am going to call the Police to remove you!"* She was loud and agitated and breathing hard.

Joe rushed past her into the living room and hurriedly rested his school bag down and got on his phone. He had started sweating as he made two calls; one to a friend who helped him to locate a place, and the other to the owner of a rental property. Within minutes he started packing his things into his RVR. Two or three trips later he had everything packed up in his friend's place across the city in Caravel Beach. Then shortly after packing them in, word came back from the property owner that he could move in that same evening and they would work out the details afterwards. Joe did, thanking his friend for coming through for him at such short notice. The RVR was reloaded a few times as retrieved his stuff which he later unpacked, this time into another, much smaller and less grand apartment on Clive Avenue.

CHAPTER 3

Those Articles

The second thing that disturbed the smooth flow of the moments in Joe's life was quite likely self-imposed. Joe loved to write, and he started getting articles published in the local Newspaper. This allowance made certain Bahamian individuals who wore titles as educators, deeply upset, simply because as a foreigner he had the guts and gall to be writing articles about life in the Bahamas, in their own Newspaper. They however, could do nothing about the written words other than read them and complain. Freedom of the Press enabled Joe to have his thoughts shared with the populace, as the Editor-in-Chief in those days got the articles into print in the only major Newspaper on the island. Joe was excited about that and enjoyed the little fame and recognition that came with it, to the extent that he had close to a dozen articles published over a six month period, covering social aspects such as Bahamian culture and music forms, issues in Education, the Bahamas as a striving nation in a changing world, Ethics and Crime, and many others. In the Ministry of Education there were persons of particular influence who thought that Joe was dabbling in their local affairs far too much, and they passed remarks publicly expressing how they felt about his writings. There was one particular article titled 'School Breaks Breaking up School' which grabbed the attention of the reading public but rubbed some educators the wrong way. In it Joe expressed that there were far too many holidays in the academic year. On the other hand, when he wrote about the need for Bahamians to be proud of their music form and put money behind its promotion, he was receiving beeps and toots when he moved about Freeport. People he didn't know called out to him on the road. From the office of District Superintendent right down to Classroom teachers, even some now dead and gone, the remarks fell on itchy ears, and then fell onto wagging tongues, which in turn churned the hot coals of rumours, propagandas and general misgivings about him and all who hailed from the land of his birth. As Joe's bravado manifested itself in the topics that he addressed in the Press, so did the dislike for him among those who already thought little of especially Jamaicans, and they did not hide their feelings when they got together to talk.

On one occasion a group of sharply dressed Bahamian men walked into a Sports Bar somewhere on one of the many islands there. They entered talking and pulled up high stools at the Bar.

One of them chuckled and said, *"I know how to do it, I know just the way to do it guys"*

"Well let's hear it then!" another responded.

"All we need to do to make a Jamaican small here is to block doors on him everywhere he turns in his bid to elevate himself, it's as simple as that guys". "Don't mind him coming here to teach with all his big Degrees and qualifications, he can never move forward or upward in this country without our consent"

The party laughed out loud, scanning the interior as they waited on their first drinks

"First thing first, monitor him really close and document everything he does that even slightly deviates from our standard requirements on his Contract" "Then blow those details out of proportion to make them appear

really big and unacceptable". "Then drop the sledge hammer on him for a misdemeanour of our choosing!" "When he appeals for forgiveness, pretend to forgive him so that you can win back his confidence". "Promise him an opportunity to demonstrate that he is reformed and willing to serve in our system again". "Then just when he thinks he can trust you again, you disappoint him big time…it will totally break his spirit, believe me!"

One of them men spoke up unexpectedly,

"Why you sounding so full of venom my brother, what these guys ever do to you so?!" glancing around the darkened room maybe to see whether they may be talking too loudly, or if there were any persons there who may recognize them, because his friend was obviously drinking before they picked him up at his place.

The loose lipped one retorted *"Ohhh,* then pausing briefly he continued, *it's obvious you not ready for this kind of conversation my friend, listen to me and listen to me good, I am a Nationalist!...Bahamians first my brother!" "These guys come here and all they do is collect a pocketful of our money and MoneyGram it*

*home to their poverty stricken country every month end,
what they know that we don't?!"*

*"But in all fairness don't they earn the money they are
sending back home bros?!...*

*"Come on man, be reasonable...Jamaica is far more
developed than the Bahamas is right now, we just set up
a University, they have UWI forever, come on,
educationally they have it over us plus the Jamaican
people put out greater interest in education than
Bahamians do!". "Don't tell me that is what you envious
about my friend!"*

*Drink your Bush Crack and try to settle down guy, we
are out here to have a good time, forget these lame-ass
Jamaicans for now.*

All over the Bar persons had turned their heads and had
been tuned in to the conversation which fortunately was
brief. One man clad in a yellow, green and black cap
slowly got up and walked out, his head staring down on
his phone screen as he texted.

"set of Jack Asses" he mumbled, glancing over his
shoulder and shaking his head as he exited the building.

The other people in the Bar were a nondescript group and they all remained zipped, keeping their opinions and accents secret. Only the drunkard squatting outside the Bar opened his frothy mouth, *"these niggas my friend are a set of ungrateful people, you cannot do anything to please them, they know dey ass friggin dumb as an ox but you thinks dey goin admit that, all dey can see is foreigners gettin'paid for jobs dey shoulda been doin, only dey not qualify to do, don't mind dem niggas my frien' leave one likkle supm wid me mek I get ma'self supm to drink man!"* saliva was dribbling down his chest as he stretched out one gnarled palm.

The man exiting dropped a five dollar note in it causing him to shout, *"HEY well modda sick, you are a GOOD MAN, yu hear mi tell yu,* he raised his shrivelled forefinger to the ceiling and then pointed it at the glass front, *"dem in dere, dey would neva do dis fo' me!"* The man looked down at him and smiled as he walked away down the road.

CHAPTER 4

Along came Rose

Joe had been separated from his wife for several months and was living at 113 Clive Avenue as the Divorce proceedings were worked through in the Magistrate Court. He still worked as a teacher in Eight Mile Rock, and attended the local Seventh Day Adventist Church. On his visits to Church he had noticed a sister named Rose. She was a beautiful dark-skinned woman with a winning smile, doe's eyes, and a sexy curvy figure. She stood about five feet and four inches in her heels and was very busy in Church activities. Somebody told him that she was actually a Deaconess. Joe enjoyed talking with her whenever he got the opportunity to do so. Then came the day that he happened to see her on the Church grounds outside of a formal service and seized the opportunity to have a conversation with her. Thereafter he offered himself to be of assistance to her, whether it was with her car, or with completing duties in the Church. They became friends and he showed her where he was living. He discovered that she worked at a placed called Bikini's Bottom and he made it a point of his duty to take her to and from work in the nights when he was able to do so. They started seeing each other romantically and a relationship developed. Joe found out that she was really not in any relationship and that she had three grown children. One Sunday afternoon she invited him to have dinner at her house and the meal was so scrumptious that he knew he had to have more meals prepared by her. He was falling in love again and she seemed happy with that. The challenge presented at this time was to find a way to keep their relationship a secret from the Church. This proved impossible but did not stop them from seeing each other. Rose allowed Joe to move into her home and he cohabited with her for about one year. The Church found out and they were subtly ostracized. Joe stopped attending regular services and Rose did her duties with less fervour than before. This illicit love nesting went on for a year before the Divorce was finalized and Joe was free. He built up the courage approximately six months later and asked her to marry him. She consented and they had a small private Ceremony at the Registrar's office during the Easter season with a few prominent members in attendance.

Suddenly they were back in the good graces of the Church. The Pastor recommended rebaptism for them, after which they were properly reintegrated into the functions and offices of the Church. The opportunity to remarry however had come at a high cost to them. On the one hand the ex-wife had continued her smear campaign against Joe and it involved Rose who she said had taken her husband from her. The ex even showed up at Church Luncheon one Sabbath afternoon fit to start a ruckus but she was quieted down by Church Elders before her tirade reached high decibels. Joe felt self-conscious whenever he came in contact with members from the branch of the Church his ex-wife attended but he never let on that he felt maligned. He did his best to show his new wife love and affection. She was not affected by the whispers and rumours because she didn't hear them and frankly would not be bothered by them as she knew she was innocent and that they were only rumours.

CHAPTER 5

Her son versus our marriage

The Divorce proceedings had been quite dramatic, because the wife, a short, almost petite Indian lady made it so by the way she went about scandalizing Joe. Apart from the fact that she had moved in friends and a lover into her apartment, the relationship had been over long before that and she had only bided her time until the perfect opportunity came along. She seized the opportunity to start a fuss when she started feeling that he didn't like her son. She was wrong. However she felt that he had dealt unfairly with her son regarding information that had come to his attention when he visited Jamaica for the Christmas Holidays in their first year of living in the Bahamas. Joe had heard when he went home that her son had thrown a stone and had broken one of the street lamps, and that the boy was mixed up with some unsavoury individuals involved in the drug trade. Joe told her over the phone what he had heard. That was the worst thing he could have done because while he was still in Jamaica she bought a ticket and flew home to get to the bottom of things in an effort to vindicate her son. Joe had been sitting in his relative's house in Cooreville Gardens one day when a vehicle pulled up at the gate and the horn sounded. He looked out and there in the passenger seat of the vehicle was his wife. She had come into the island and had gone and met with the individuals her husband had told her about, who from all indications turned out to be fine people in her estimation. She introduced the driver and other occupants as the individuals with whom her son had been hanging out, expounding that they were really just nice people and that Joe's presumptions about them were simply that, presumptions. She had done her dirt and Joe really felt stupid. Whether Joe held on to his hurt ego or not, things never got back to normal after that incident. The Holidays ended and they returned to the Bahamas on separate flights. From that return to the Bahamas the marriage took a downward turn. One argument followed the other and the previously reported exploits of her son was at the centre of each of them. Things climaxed one Friday afternoon when news of her rumours about Joe reached the ears of the District Superintendent. He sent instructions to have her immediately transferred from the School where they both worked to another High School on the island. She had to report there the following Monday. She moved out of the apartment that same afternoon and went to stay with a colleague of hers at some place unknown to Joe. She continued her tirade by placing Joe in the Magistrate Court claiming for a percentage of the Rent that the Bahamian Government made available to him. The Magistrate was able to see through her antics, especially toward the end of the divorce proceedings when she showed up in Court dressed in a black and white suit and responding to her questions by speaking in old English. The Divorce was granted while the claim for Rental assistance was dismissed. Joe sighed in relief and sobbed quietly as he went out the doors of the Courthouse toward his car.

CHAPTER 6

The Walden Masters and the Principal

The fourth thing that transpired was positive. It was really the best thing for Joe to have done to return to feeling like his life was worth living. He saw an advertisement about Walden University on Facebook as he browsed one evening and immediately clicked on it. He registered in the university and undertook a Master of Science Degree with specialization in Educational Leadership. He completed this program online over a two year period, completing the Internship and graduating with a 3.9 GPA in December of 2013. This Degree was qualification to become an Educational Leader, an improvement on what used to be 'Principal'. He was hyped up and quietly anticipated the day when he would serve at the helm of an educational institution and get to guide the various structures that makes it successful. At this same time a self-proclaimed Nationalist was in his ascendancy to become Principal at the school where Joe worked. This man will remain nameless as a result of the author's fear of being falsely accused of making libellous statements. The man was obviously highly upset about his subordinate, a foreigner, attempting to earn himself a Masters Degree, even though the Department of Education requires that teachers constantly upgrade themselves academically to remain relevant in the classroom. He looked for opportunities to mar Joe's name on the campus where he was then Vice-Principal, and he got the opportunity in the following way:

It happened that one day he walked into Joe's classroom and heard music coming from an inner room there. He enquired about the sounds as Joe went to turn the music down. Joe had been playing the jazzy sound track of a game, "100 Hidden Objects" padap pap paada, padap pap pap pap, pap, pap, pap, pap, pap, pap paada, papappaada!…'on his Laptop which he had connected to additional speakers he had brought to School. Joe told him that he had been playing music when he stepped into the doorway of the inner room and saw the Laptop. Mind you, there were no students in the classroom at the time because Joe was not scheduled for a class at the time.

The gentleman, if he may truthfully be addressed as such, went away claiming that he had caught Joe working on his Masters Degree in class, during class time, and ignoring the students there. A group of boys who had been hanging around outside of Joe's classroom in the absence of their Air-Conditioning and Refrigeration teacher, were committed to memory as students who should have been in Joe's class but whom he had allowed to be outside wasting time; this to be used as evidence of his lack of care for them.

CHAPTER 7

Broken Wrist, Principal, and NIB

The actions of the nameless one must have been born of jealousy as previously alluded to because some months later, when a student threw a rock and broke Joe's wrist while trying to injure another boy in a brawl, the gentleman refused to believe that Joe had been injured even after being informed of the rock throwing incident by other members of staff. Eventually he conceded, saying, *"okay, since Joe wants to be a cry baby...."*

Joe had to go to the Hospital to have his right wrist set later that day, this after another big-headed, short man who people knew as a Doctor at the local Clinic sew up the skin on Joe's wrist and told him he would be okay. In that moment Joe made the mistake of asking the Doctor,

"Do you think it would be wise to get a second opinion about my wrist doc?!"

The short Medical Practitioner paused and stared at him as if he had blasphemed. *"Are you second guessing my ability as a Surgeon here Mr. Shelteroch, I cant believe you, why would you even ask me such a question, how dare you?!"* he hung his Stethoscope around his neck and stomped away fuming. An examination carried out at the Rand that afternoon revealed that the wrist had indeed been broken; the second opinion paid off.

As demonstrated by the Vice-Principal, it could be concluded that jealousy and narrow-mindedness can be a weight on a body, that narrow-mindedness is very common among small-island people and that it gets to be that weight if a body is not Bahamian by birth.

Joe during his tenure was to meet and relate to a few of these weight-impacting individuals who inadvertently exposed themselves as a group of individuals who network between New Providence and the rest of the Bahamas. Somebody who works as a Filing Clerk, another person who answers the telephone and takes messages, one person who works in the Payroll Department or Treasury, and the person with the dark agenda is all that is required to make the process work. Their mission it was, and maybe still is, to thwart the efforts of ex-pat teachers; the ones who refuse to roll over for them and wag tails like puppies in their line of duty. Miniscule misunderstandings are blown out of proportion and end up on the permanent files of the foreigners, to the merriment of those involved in the underhanded practice. Speaking up for one's self as a foreigner was usually deemed as insubordination on their part, even when they were in the right about the issues they spoke up about. When Joe began experiencing the dark side of unscrupulous elements inside the Department of Education, he knew that it was founded in small-mindedness on their part regarding the fact that foreigners were doing jobs that Bahamians should be doing. It only confirmed and exposed certain underlying realities that he had suspected long before: foreigners, especially Jamaicans, are envied simply because they are smart and capable people who exert themselves and get things done in an environment where indolence is almost deified.

CHAPTER 8

Going DOWN anyone, Joe is!

To back up briefly, Joe had gotten his wrist broken by a student on the school grounds. Joe had been standing that fateful day, having a discussion with the young lady who worked as Guidance Counsellor at the time, outside the Carpentry Shop on the campus. Two boys who obviously had a disagreement which they had deemed serious enough to be escalated into a fight, was conducting their unruly business instead of being inside whichever class they should have been. One boy it seems had run away from the other, placing them on either side of the Carpentry building. Joe was by then standing in front of the Carpentry building in discussion with the Guidance Counsellor when a boy ran towards them and stood, using their bodies as a shield. Joe being an alert individual thought it strange that the boy just came and stood there beside them so he glanced around just in time to see another boy rushing towards them from the other side of the building. He had a big rock in his hand which he threw with all his might in the direction of Joe, the

Guidance Counsellor and his adversary. The rock connected squarely with Joe's right wrist and broke it. It was an accident but one worthy of a caning, the involvement of the Police and a suspension. The boy was merely suspended for two weeks while Joe suffered and could have been dismissed from his job for failure to report to work. This is how life unfolded for Joe after that unfortunate incident. Joe was advised to report the matter to the National Insurance Board (NIB) by the medical personnel who attended to him in the Hospital. He did and was given Forms to fill in describing the way in which he became injured. He complied and was awarded just under $400.00 per forth-night for three months. This access to National Insurance Board assistance was most infuriating for certain individuals in privileged positions. His broken wrist meant absolutely nothing to them. If you have ever seen a set of angry people; angry, educated people, Joe saw them and was exposed to their dignified wrath. They launched an investigation into whether Joe was guilty of wrong doing, 'double-dipping' as it is called when an individual is deemed to be getting paid by the Government via dual channels for doing the same job. The unnamed Vice-Principal gentleman and a group of others of like minds set about monitoring the movements Joe made while wearing the Cast on his right forearm. He was stalked at another institution where he had been doing an hour in the mornings, before School time, three days per week for a number of years. Joe was called in at the end of his recovery period when he returned to School and accused of, yes you guessed it, double-dipping. They told him how he had been stealing from the Bahamian Government by continuing to work at the 'secondary' institution and getting paid for doing so, while refusing to turn up for work at his regular job on the grounds that he had a broken wrist. Their argument was questioning how it was that he was able to turn up at the secondary location but could not turn up at his regular job site to do the job he was employed in the Bahamas to do.

In a emergency meeting one day the Principal queried *"Mr. Shelteroch I have evidence that you are working in Freeport while pretending to be unable to come to work here, why is that?!"*

The District Superintendent who was the third person in the office, stared at the Joe as the question was asked.

"I won't deny that I still help out the Boatyard Trainees at that place in Freeport, I am not hiding that sir, I am happy to be assisting in enabling young Bahamians to face the future!"

She entered the conversation now, *"so then, tell us why you are able to go there but fail to come and do the job that you have been employed to do at this institution?!"*

"Mrs. Roper, Mr.Shuffler, frankly, Technical Drawing, which I teach in town, requires no stress on my limbs to execute. I am required to operate machinery and equipment here, lift and carry lumber around the Workshop here, among other strenuous activities, which would be impossible with this Cast on my arm, which is why I don't report for work, and please remember that I had been given time off to recover from my injury as well, please, until the end of March" Joe stared from one face to the other and back as he defended himself.

"which is why I am here now, my wrist has healed and I am back to work"

"Anyhow, we have heard you, just understand that this kind of thing is called 'double-dipping' and it is frowned upon by Government here brother"

"but Mr. Shuffler are you saying you would have preferred those Bahamian students in that Boatyard Training Program to be without an instructor for the duration of my healing because I was earning a few extra dollars there, because that sounds very strange to me coming from an educated person. I was concerned about them completing the Program they were doing, that's why I showed up there, because as it was I was not indisposed since I hardly needed to use my hand in executing my instructions to them in Technical Drawing class, that's it sir!"

"Mr. Shelteroch you may go now, we have heard enough from you today, you will be hearing from us again" Joe got up and walked out, closing the door behind him.

The reality was that whereas Joe taught Technical Drawing at the part-time job, which required little or no strain on his limbs, he would have had to operate heavy-duty machines and equipment on his full time job, which his broken wrist would not have handled without causing further, and maybe even permanent damage to his wrist.

Joe settled back into his regular job in accordance with Government Policy via the National Insurance Board. However, shortly after that meeting with the Principal and District Superintendent he wrote and submitted a letter informing him that he would be resigning and returning home to Jamaica at the end of that School year. This was 2014. Joe had returned to the job in April. The Principal now knew that he had lost a teacher and wondered whether he had been the cause of it. He summoned Joe to his office one day and asked him, *"Mr. Shelteroch I received your letter yesterday, stating your intention to resign at the end of the school year"* Joe nodded, *"that is true sir"*

"I just need you to tell me if I am the reason you have decided to resign at this time Mr. Shelteroch" he stared at Joe as he enquired.

"No, No, No Mr. Shuffler, that was my plan from the time I came to the Bahamas. I turn fifty this year and I had told myself back then that I would return home when I reach this age, nothing to do with you at all Mr. Shuffler!" Joe stared blankly back at him across the desk.

CHAPTER 9

The Wrong Name!

The summer came and Joe moved back to Jamaica with high hopes of resettling in his homeland. He saw an ad in a local Newspaper and applied early in the month of August. He was called to an interview at Kingston College. He was there ahead of the 11:00 A.M. appointment and obviously interviewed well because later that afternoon he received a message telling him congratulations and welcoming him to his new job. That school year started and Joe discovered that there was a problem looming.

The Bursar called him in one day, *"good morning Mr. Shelteroch!"* The Bursar was a man of medium height and light complexion. He always dressed sharp. This morning he was wearing a white shirt with a purple tie and black trousers and looking dapper as ever. Joe hoped to hear positive things from him.

"How are you sir Kentle?!" he returned the greetings. The Bursar pointed to a chair and he sat down. *"Mr.*

Shelteroch I received your email yesterday, nice shirt by the way", he pointed at Joe and smiled, "yes, and I checked with the Ministry regarding the issue you described. They told me that they cannot pay you for the Masters Degree in your first year here but next year your salary will be adjusted"

"what about years of service then, I have been working consistently for the past twenty odd years. I should be at the top of the scale by now don't you think so?!"

Mr. Kentle hung his head, "you are correct sir but I can only tell you what they told me."

Joe was highly disappointed at this time, "What can I do now Mister Kentle, we both know the dollar here doesn't stretch very far. I am afraid I won't be able to meet my bills at the end of the month, my rent alone is $40,000.00. By the way, if I may ask, how much I am to expect this month end, do you know?!"

"I will call the Ministry later today and find out for you okay. Call me or come and see me before this week ends okay, I should hear something by then, okay". He pushed back his chair and got up, *"I have to step out for a few minutes, so take care, and remember to get in touch with me!"* Both men walked out of the small office and Joe headed toward his vehicle. Mr. Kentle disappeared into the Principal's office across the hallway.

Friday morning Joe got a call from the Bursar informing him that he needed to produce proof that he is really Joseph Shelteroch.

"They want you to bring in your Birth Certificate so they may match the spelling of your names to the spelling on some of your Certificates on file. Take the Birth Certificate directly to the Ministry, building #3, okay, the earlier the better okay" the voice squeaked through the cell phone.

"okay sir Kentle, I hope I can find the time to get down there on Monday since I didn't carry my Birth Certificate with me today, thanks very much", Joe hung up and dropped the phone into his pocket.

Joe had to miss school that Monday to conduct his business at Ministry of Education. Speak about slow and the absence of a personal touch in customer service and they were present at the Ministry. Joe reflected on the way he had frowned at the Bahamian system as being slow compared to Jamaica but now he had to wonder which was really slower. So much had changed in the country since the beginning of the new millennium though. The Ministry now hired lower level staff with a view to save on salary and wages payout and this resulted in a poorer quality of service to the public. High School graduates who did not do well enough to enter into a job making real money and providing a meaningful contribution to the development of the nation got jobs in Customer Service at the MOE. These young people slouched on the job and were often unaccounted for at the desk they should be occupying, making visiting for business a scary prospect. Precious time is always lost with nothing positive to show for it. At least in Freeport the journey to the Ministry was much shorter and one didn't have to contend with the heat and traffic as it is in Kingston. Thereafter Joe had to submit his Degree Certificate to be copied. The copy had to be forwarded to two the Joint Board of Teacher Education, and the Education Council of Jamaica which were at different locations in the city. Tedious is not the most suitable word to describe getting around Kingston when one is strapped for time. The traffic is a nightmare all through the day. Several visits to the Ministry and several months later Joe still had not gotten any solution to the issue with the spelling of his name. He had only discovered that the spelling of his name on his Master of Science Degree was different from the spelling on his Mico Diploma. He knew how that came to be but his word was not enough to have any change made or to render the Masters acceptable. Eventually he wrote the Ministry and explained to them what had happened, but by then a whole year had passed and he had had to survive on a skeleton budget. He had also been offered a job back in the Bahamas.

CHAPTER 10

Back to the Bahamas again!

A day came when Joe received an email from the secondary institution he had worked in the Bahamas, inviting him to return there and take up a position there as an instructor. He had grown discontented and frustrated working at Kingston College and having to relate to the Ministry of Education and so he was excited and jumped on the opportunity. By the first week of August he was in the Bahamas and started working on the 15th of the month. He was able to be with his wife and attend Church again with the brethren there and so he ignored the fact that he really loved his country more. The salary for this new job was the best he had ever been paid and to top it off he was being paid bi-monthly. Every two weeks he was collecting a check, as unbelievable as it seemed. This job went on fine even though Joe had to work odd hours including nights and on the weekend. He worked with it for two years, enjoying stints of administrative function in the process, something he privately yearned for. Toward the end of two years he started having inklings of returning to work in the Government system. The devil must have been in the workings here. Joe made enquires and was eventually told by his former Principal, after a verbal beat down in a crowded and public setting, that he could go ahead and apply and he would see to it that he gets employed. If Joe had paid close attention to his body language as he spoke he would not have trusted in him because unknown to Joe he had been baited and had swallowed the hook with it.

CHAPTER 11

A 6 for a 9

What happened next is almost too evil to speak about.
Joe was invited to the meeting of new teachers late in the
month of August of 2018, after resigning his position at
the secondary institution he had returned to, in
confidence that he would be employed with the MOE.
He sat through that meeting and heard all that was said.
He was then told by the same Principal gentleman, that
he had been posted to a particular School on the island.
Joe turned up at that School and attended the campus for
three days before he was called into the Principal's
office and cautiously advised not to begin signing the
daily Register until they had received his official letter of
Appointment.

*The Fisherman had tugged at the line and the hook
penetrated Joe's flesh.*

That appointment letter never came up to the end of that
September. Then Joe received a phone call from

somebody in Nassau requesting his email address. Joe thought it strange that the official channels in Nassau did not already have his email address but he gave it to the person as requested. Shortly afterwards, maybe a day later he received an email message stating that the Department of Education regrets to inform him that 'they were unable to offer him employment at this time'. Joe was crestfallen, highly disappointed and deeply hurt by that reality. He had been 'done right in' as a Bahamian song rightly puts it. A subversive group of 'educators' had cunningly plotted and gotten him to resign his job, encouraged by the promise of a job back in the MOE. Now Joe was without a job and undoubtedly the conspirators all had a good laugh, in private. Joe the metaphoric fish, had been caught and pulled out of the water, out of the stream of Bahamian money, now to gasp for air-without a job- until he died, unless...

CHAPTER 12

And it's back to Jamaica again!

Joe moved back to Jamaica a second time, leaving his wife in the Bahamas; not that the tearing apart of his family was any concern of those underhanded individuals as they had plotted and schemed and chuckled about it, maybe over Kalik or Sands Beer.

God had remained faithful to him and this time he got a job in the original Capital of Spanish Town. He interviewed for this job via Skype, was successful, and started working on the 8th of October 2018. After a fairly successful year there, during which he stabilized the Carpentry Department, prepared students for CSEC and City and Guilds programs and exams, Joe was ready to move on again. He had gotten exposed to the Jamaican version of bigotry manifested in members of his Department out of fear that he would be assigned as their next H.O.D. The H.O.D had proved to be lacking in experience and necessary skills and leadership was aware of it. Joe had also become quite tense as he realized that his workplace was really situated in an area where violent things could happen at just about any moment without warning. The male students were all mini-soldiers-in-waiting, waiting to join the ranks of those that the Constabulary and Special Forces hunted. The campus was a squeezed up space that the students did nothing to keep clean and so when these factors were all pulled together in his cranium Joe was mentally ready to leave. He was frustrated by the insufficient attention paid to the Department by the School leadership and by the snail-paced approach to the adjusting of his salary by the Ministry of Education. Like the previous time when he had returned to Jamaica and worked in the vicinity of North Street at that popular All-Boys High School, the academic year had passed again without him being properly sorted out in regard to his proper salary being paid to him. It almost felt as if he was not a Jamaican, in his own country.

And so, withstanding the fact that he had acquired a car with a Teachers Credit Union Loan which he would now have to pay off without enjoying the benefit of the vehicle, he returned once again to the Bahamas, leaving the car with his youngest daughter, having decided to respond to a nagging feeling he was having of doing the right and proper thing and placing himself in the same space with his wife. Doing so he knew, would also be bringing an end to his lonely, messed up life of turbulent nights and loud music. Joe returned on the 7th of July 2019 to his wife and remains there to this day, working at a small private Methodist institution.

CHAPTER 13

Man Down; JOE!!!

Meanwhile, and as the clock tocked, four men entered a Bar somewhere in the downtown area of Freeport, on the Bahamian island of Grand Bahama, carrying cans and bottles from which they sipped dark fluids. They belched one after the other, loudly as they staggered across to the farthest section away from the entrance. They must have been patrons because the Bouncer at the door did not stop them from entering. Sitting at the Bar counter were other men and among them one woman. They knew the drunks and they watched them take their seats at the back, curious to hear what they were babbling about this time around.

"Yes I is see him 'roun' di place, knockin' bout pawdie, yu see I sayin', good good man who cum eya' from his country to teach deze Bahamian kids, I does see him, yu see I sayin'. And I ere he was a fine teacha too, yu see I sayin' but dem niggas inside dat same Ministry, what dey call it, ahhh, Ministry of Edumucation, yes

*somebaddy in dere mess him up big time yu see I sayin',
I tellin' you how it go bros!"*

*"what I ere is dat he use to push up hissef too much in
Bahamian business, das what I ere!"*

The third of the fourth made his entrance, *"yall is be
drinkin' an when yu is drink yu is be talkin' all type a
garbage roun' eya, let me break it down fo you bai, da
man, da same nigga de whe' he is right now because one
nigga, one short nigga who dey have inside dat aahhmm,
Ministry, envious of him 'cause he gone do Masters
Degree before him and keep usin' big words when dey is
be talkin bai, das all dat is, da man set some odda people
in Nassau on him an dey conspire to write him up an put
bad tings on his file in Nassau, I know wha I sayin bros,
not tellin' yu a word a lie!"* He slapped the table hard
and leaned back in his chair, beard wet and eyes rolling
around shiny as a full moon.

*"Da one deeaadd, da one dead buddy, well mudda sick,
dey do him bad hey, mudda sickin!"*

"is all these bad ways we got cause da Dorian hurricane half kill we yu know bai, I serious!"

"is time we give dem flickin yaad people an dem ai'tian people a break if yu aks mi buddy, tings ain lookin' too good roun' eya, da man shoulda neva lose he likkle wok bai!"

The men chatted on oblivious to the audience they had, until their containers were empty, then they stood up, groggy from too much alcohol, and staggered back out into the night, belching and farting almost rhythmically as they went.

As a man now, Joe feels himself diminished, like a bright light hidden by very thick drapes behind the elevated stage of a grand Concert Hall, and he has been effectively diminished by the characters mentioned throughout this short story so far. He is there in the Bahamas, known by those who worked their 'witchcraft' on him, and by extension known by just about every other Bahamian because news and especially gossip gets around mighty quickly in small island communities. He is there with his Masters Degree, his twenty-odd years of experience and expertise, his track record of producing successful students and favourable passes in the National examinations; sitting there with his pride badly hurt as the world turns favourably for those underhanded dealers who are considered educators. Imagine a mindset that exalts what the teacher is paid above what the teacher imparts to the students. Imagine a mindset that finds it impossible to praise anything creative that a foreign teacher may do on any day. Imagine a mindset that fails to see the coordinated effort of all the stakeholders as they enable students in their quest for an education, and instead is only able to see a foreign teacher earning a few extra dollars. True educators do not possess that kind of mindset anywhere in the world. Imagine such individuals driving around aware of the wrong they do to people every year and then, try to figure whether they sleep peacefully at nights. Obviously they do because there is no gossip going around saying they aren't. Joe is a diminished man residing in a strange land now, lost as it were, clinging dearly to the reduced salary that his latest job pays him. He feels ashamed of his diminished status among his now invisible former MOE colleagues.

However, as dark and foreboding the skies above Joe's head may seem to be, he is not nearly perturbed. In fact, and remaining true to his name and nature, Joe is looking around for opportunities, a way of escape, and escape to anywhere, preferably outside of the third world and its restrictive realities. In his mind he has reconciled with himself regarding the ways in which he may be held responsible for the way things turned out; those articles in the newspaper, talking up for himself on the occasions that he did and so on, had certainly been seeds sown that had germinated and had borne a full harvest in his life. At the same time Joe remembers the evil hand he had been dealt by the small group of conspirators within the Department of Education and secretly hopes for the day when they and others like them will be totally removed from the education system so that the sun may shine in, on all those who serve, regardless of their origins, race or nationality.

As a child of God Joe is grateful to the heavenly father for keeping him employed continuously as he made his sojourn back and forth between the Bahamas and Jamaica. He is grateful for good health and guidance from above. Even when he conducted himself contrary to God's will for his life and got into troubling times filled with phobias and fears too numerous and disgusting to even disclose, God had remained faithful. Joe is thankful that in spite of the obvious let down by the Bahamian system that he served faithfully for almost twelve years, that there are still individuals who will share a smile with him and a moment of humour. He is grateful that his body still functions effectively and that his senses remain sharp and fairly keen. He is also very grateful to God that evil people have walked different paths from his so that there have not been any encounters with gunmen, shootouts, kidnappings, diseases, or vehicular accidents. Joe is thankful that he is aware enough to realize that God is above all of his circumstances. He has accepted that God deserves some of his time instead of him consuming every moment, thinking about the wrongs meted out to him. He is happy that money has never been the driving force in his life, as necessary as it is. He is however still ambitious and patient, hoping that as time passes and things unfolds, he will get to realize his true and full potential in this life as God grants him days here.

One essential truth that has been made plain here is that people will usually do the things they realize that they can do to those they realize that they are able to do those things to as long as there is no fear of being made accountable subsequently. Sadly, when that freedom to do what is possible is abused by individuals who harbour hate and envy and jealousy in their hearts, others like Joe will suffer. That's just how it is. Joe I am certain has learnt his lesson.

The End

DORIAN CLIMBS A MOUNTAIN

One couple's experience during and after Hurricane Dorian

By: Sez Hoo

One day a large Boulder became loose on the side of a great mountain and rolled down the side of the mountain, eventually slamming and coming to rest in the river down in the valley. The boulder was so big that it stopped the river from flowing on down slope as it had done for centuries. Now there are some people that live along the banks of the river and relied on the river for their livelihood. When the boulder blocked the river many of them packed up their belongings and moved far up the mountainside to resettle. Many however chose to remain. Some of them said, *"ah well, at least that large*

Boulder is no longer up on the mountain so it cannot roll down another time". Others said, "boulders like these only come loose every couple Centuries, so we will be long gone before another one rolls down. However, among the people there lived a wise old man by the name of Dorian, wrinkled all over his body and with hair as white as snow. One day he hobbled into the village square and started talking with the folks he saw there. He told them that the village is not a safe place to live and that everyone should relocate further up the mountain, but they laughed at him. Anyway, before leaving the square he invited everybody to walk with him to the river as he had something interesting to show them. When they got to the river the old man climbed to an elevated point along the bank and pointed toward the massive boulder.

" Look carefully!" He said, *"notice the base of the*
boulder!". "The river's constant flow is gradually moving
small particles from around the base of the boulder and
one day this boulder will roll further down the river!".
"If that happens all of us who live in that village down
there will die, don't say I didn't warn you!".

With that, the old man turned and hobbled back down
the hill toward his small house in the village. The crowd
followed and watched him enter the small thatched
house he lived in, before they turned away to head back
to the square. As they turned however, they noticed that
the old man was coming back out of his house. This time
he had a bundle hung over one shoulder and a tall
walking stick in the other. He slowly walked by the
gathering and headed back up slope toward the place
they had just returned from. He did not say a word to

anyone. He just walked on, out of their sight, and when he came to the boulder, he did not stop there either. With one backward glance he began his journey further up the mountain until he was totally lost from view.

Many, many years later the unexpected happened: the boulder had finally been unearthed from its settling spot by river erosion and down the river it rolled until it somehow rolled over a low bank and out of the riverbed. What happened next was simply unbelievable. The river gushed down like a Tsunami and flooded the entire village.

Like the alter-ego or nemesis of the character Dorian in the epilogue, Hurricane Dorian struck the island chain of the Bahamas on September 1, 2019, travelling from the east. The island of Abaco was submerged in waves and then its low terrain scraped of human life. Hundreds, maybe even thousands of persons lost their lives according to the News Reports while many hundreds are still missing. Like the old man's warning was spurned, so has the people of the Bahamas spurned the warnings and commentary that points out that the archipelago is very low, and that with it being in the middle of the ocean, catastrophic flooding is possible whenever there is any major weather system within the Caribbean basin. It has been reported that the island of Grand Bahama was approximately 75 percent under water as a result of hurricane Dorian as well and several people died there from drowning.

Rising sea levels and low-lying lands like the Bahamas share a sad refrain sung in duet. The one a wail, and the other a scream. The wail- of dying souls: the scream- of punishing winds, and angry waves. Dorian's warning long ignored by the village folks had borne poisonous fruit and they were drowning in the frothing waters of the inundated river.

The 48 hours from September 1, 2019 to September 2, 2019 will not ever be forgotten by the people living in the Bahamas, especially those residing in the islands of Abaco and Grand Bahama. Sunday September 1 was the end of a waiting period for the Bahamian people. For at least eight days they had been hearing of a system developing in the region, from a Tropical Storm status to a Category 1 hurricane. Then from a Category 1 hurricane to a Category 2 hurricane, then from a Category 2 hurricane to a Category 3 hurricane. The system continued to strengthen to become a Category 4 hurricane and then to a Category 5 hurricane. The people prayed and hoped that the system would turn away from the islands and weaken as it travelled over the waters, but it didn't.

The howling started in the afternoon of Sunday September 1st. and with it came an unusual dread that could not be readily identified, just an unusual feeling, a premonition of sorts. On Grand Bahama the newscasts were not coming because the Telecommunications systems providers had turned off their equipment to protect them from what they suspected was about to unfold in the region. As news filtered in from Abaco the dread heightened among the residents, but then as night began to fall the electricity was turned off. Now it was totally impossible for the people to get any updates on what was happening. The residents were like sitting ducks. Maybe those who had lived on the island for long periods of time may have had a better understanding of what was possible, but they remained and hoped.

Without the radio stations, and the electricity turned off, the people thought they had seen the worst but then the water supply was also turned off by the Commission, to preserve its equipment and minimize contamination. It would now be up to each resident to employ survival skills in this hour of uncertainty. Nobody knew how strong the system had become, or whether it was weakening or strengthening even further. Then the access to internet was interrupted and subsequently turned off as conditions worsened. The people waited, hoping against hope that Dorian would do what so many previous hurricanes had done, and drift to the north or south of the archipelago. Night darkened but many people did not go to sleep. The fear was heavy like a damp cloth on the heads of all. The people who were able to hear any news kept hearing how badly Abaco was being damaged by the hurricane, which was said to have slowed to a mere crawl. This was a dangerous sign. Dorian continued to slow down until it was moving, barely crawling along the seas toward Grand Bahama. News was sketchy concerning Abaco by then, so the people only hoped for the best for their relatives living there.

Toward mid-morning on Monday September 2nd the water came. It just crested the highest points on Grand Bahama and rushed inland from almost every angle. To this day it still strikes me as strange the way the water engulfed some areas and by-passed others on the similar landscapes. The residents of # 68 East Coral Close rushed out of the house, barely grabbing anything with them other than the key to the car. They managed to lift a chair or two off the floor onto a bed and placed a few items of clothing and some shoes on top of another bed and they were gone, totally forgetting about important documents other than those the wife had always kept in her handbag. There were three individuals living in that home and when the alert was sounded by the youngest, the son, they rushed to the front door only to see the water, about a foot high, rapidly flowing down the gentle slope on which their house was situated. They just about panicked and frantically took the working vehicle out of the yard where it had been moored the previous evening to protect it from high winds. This would now be their saviour from the invading flood. The winds had died down and the waters were claiming land by the second. The water quickly filled up the low-lying places in the parking lot outside the house and flowed around into the yard. They decided as a family that the Rental should be parked and left on the premises of the Central Church of God. With that being agreed the husband got into the small Rental and drove behind his wife who drove the Bb, through a neighbour's yard and over to the Church. They did not battle the idea of calling out to their neighbours for more than a few seconds because everybody was battened up inside their houses across the road and on either side of # 68. For a fleeting moment the wife wanted to call out to the neighbours, but the husband disagreed with the idea because of the un-neighbourliness of the folks under normal conditions. He did not know whether their effort to reach out to them would be appreciated and so they had driven off, heading across to the Church with the high blue top. The son drove out in his personal car and they parted company at the gate of the Church as both wife and husband brought both vehicles into that premises. The husband parked the small Rental and joined his wife inside the Bb. Opening and closing the doors was a challenge as the wind was unpredictable and would howl for a few seconds and then just as quickly subside. Coral road was near impassable by this time and the water was rippling with waves reminiscent of incoming tide when one is at the beach. Inside the Church yard several other vehicles were already parked as the owners huddled inside to shelter from the hurricane. They were to be there for quite a long while. A few moments after arriving the wife suggested that they leave the Church premises and try to get downtown to her place of business, maybe that area would fare better than where they were. They made it across Coral road and maybe another two hundred feet up on Pioneers Way before deciding to turn around and head back. The road was already inundated with water as high as the tire and a number of vehicles had shut down in the water ahead of them; a Yellow School Bus and several Trucks. They turned around, gas Tank on two strokes from empty and headed back to the Central Church with the high blue top. They rolled and drifted into the premises slowly so as not to agitate the water and cause it to get inside the vehicle. The son had gone out of their sight and was hopefully doing his best to negotiate to somewhere less inundated. After a few minutes the wife made the decision to head down to the Freeport Seventh Day Adventist Church, off Gambier Drive. They headed there and were able to brace against the wind and rain to get in through the door which was manned by community folks who had been allowed to use the facility as a Shelter. After sitting on chairs for what seemed like a very long time the couple, obviously nervous and restless in their spirits left the Shelter and went back out to the Bb. They stayed in the vehicle for approximately one hour, feeling it bouncing on the different tires as strong winds buffeted the Church grounds. Thankfully no water flowed onto the sacred grounds. They watched from inside the Bb as the building took its beating and lost roofing material in sheets. They worried about a BMW that had been parked, supposedly in the shadow of the building for protection, because they noticed how vulnerable it was, parked under the eave, the part of the building taking most of the battering. Eventually they went back inside, accepting a stiff rebuke at the door with candour. It was getting close to the end of another day, but it was hard to tell without checking the screen of a cellular phone. Everywhere was grey and the wind was howling. It continued to howl, unabated until they decided to make their way through the thickening, excited, scared crowd, wet and distressed, to the inner Sanctuary where they had been instructed to go hours earlier. Through the door that separated the Sanctuary from the Fellowship Hall they went, slipping and sliding around persons lounging wherever they found a space, up against a wall, or on the floor somewhere. They apologised as they stepped over curled up bodies, some wrapped from head to toe, some already sleeping in the semi-darkness of the Church building. There was quite a bit of chatter as individuals and family members kept each other's spirits up. Lights from Cellular phones and Tablets spotted the growing darkness as people held their heads down for whatever sliver of entertainment or news updates they could access. Some persons had chosen to climb up on the rostrum where the Choir sits during Worship and were huddled there in groups, chatting wildly. The couple from #68 East Coral Close found seats somewhere in the middle of the building and started settling down for the night. They comforted each other as best they could, trying their best to remain calm in the stressful situation. They listened to the conversations going on all over the interior but did not try to make sense of any of it, other than those that contained details about the hurricane. As the night progressed a few things happened: Somebody assumedly in charge announced over the din that they were asking the people bundled up on the platform to remove themselves and allow only elderly folks and mothers with young children to occupy that space. After much mumbling and expressions of disgust and resentment for the lonely voice, persons started to move down and the elderly and mothers moved into their places. The second thing that happened was the voice of a woman that rose above the chattering crowd in a spirit of praise to Almighty God for having taken her through the years and turning her life around from one of harlotry to becoming a born-again Christian. The woman marched, maybe pranced a bit, up and down the aisle relating her dubious past without shame and claiming that she was, back in the day, Freeport's best nightwalker in the process. She confessed to the husbands she had conducted liaisons with and the grief she know she must have brought to families but then she thanked God for bringing her to her senses and sparing her life to see his goodness after her turn-around. She carried on with her sermon for the better part of a half an hour and then she subsided and stopped. Moments later a male voice picked up on what started off as a similar train of thought, to bring comfort to the hurting, frightened state of mind that most persons must have been experiencing, but he gradually altered his discourse to one in which he was begging for money, admitting that he was willing to accept whatever anyone in the building would make available to him right there on the spot. Following his short attempt at testifying, which turned out to be nothing more than a bit of testilying as one of my Church brothers often said, another female stood up, this time somewhere up on the elevated Rostrum. She gave a brief testimony of herself and how God had kept her, before bursting into a song of praise. Her contribution was applauded and the couple from #68

East Coral close even said an Amen at the end of her presentation.

The night must have been wearing on, but it was hard to say because despite the attempts by individuals to stay positive, the wind just kept on howling. It had started lifting and slamming some part of the roof of the Fellowship Hall now and so the ears of the captive congregation were constantly being barraged by the windy onslaught. It sounded like somebody using a Cricket Bat to vehemently beat against a zinc fence, or like a mighty threshing machine. I guess it was sounding exactly like what it was, the devastating winds of historic hurricane Dorian, dismantling the roof of a Fellowship Hall. The couple entertained a few brief conversations with ghostly faces in the dark until gradually, slowly the talking died down and people drifted off to sleep, leaving the blue-screen addicts to search the internet for whatever they search for, the blue lights of their screens exposing in its light, whatever dust particles there were present in the enclosure of the building. It became quiet inside, a little, as the couple tried to relax into sleep. The wife succeeded for a while, laying her upper body across the lap of her husband who was sitting up straight in one of the pews. As he sat there supporting her, he dozed off and enjoyed a few winks, only to be awakened every time she adjusted her body on his thigh. Eventually she woke and sat up, offering to return the favour. He accepted and relaxed his upper frame on her thighs. He endured the comfort possible there for a short period and then slid his body down to the carpet. There he folded himself into a space as comfortable as he could and fell asleep. When he had dozed for maybe an hour he awoke, and his wife went down. She might have gone down first, I am not a hundred percent certain, but they both slept for a while on the carpet.

Things were not going as well for elderly folks, especially one old man who started calling out for somebody by their name. No one seem to know who he was, or the person he was calling out to, because nobody responded. He shuffled his way through the pews as though searching for his friend. His backside was soaked in urine and as he passed by everybody knew he had wet himself. The old man seemed disoriented several minutes later when he tried to find his way back to where he was seated before. He kept starting into one pew after another and then changing his mind. Somebody eventually led him by his hand and sat him down in a pew that had space. He laid there, all soaked and smelling, but such was life for those of us close to him. There was the occasional fart to take the mind off the banging roof metal, and in a similar way the snoring of those who snore, as they went through their sleep cycle on the carpet.

At one time the couple checked their phone and discovered that it was just after midnight. It should have been closer to dawn by then, but it seemed time was simply moving so much slower.

They dozed off again. Maybe everybody dozed off, finally tuning out the banging of the loose roof sheeting against the roof framing members, the farting, and the snoring, as they accepted that Dorian was bent on continuing its punishing act.

The next time they woke it was after 5:00 in the morning. Inspecting their reality, they realised they were no worse for wear than when they moved into the Shelter almost a day ago. As a result, they decided to start the new day, together.

They got up from the pew shortly before 6:00 and headed outside. The strong gusts of wind had stopped, and the roof was quiet above the Fellowship Hall. The sky was becoming light as they entered the Bb and sat for a moment to assess the damage incurred during the night. The BMW under the eave had been smashed by a part of the roof that fell on it. There were other portions of the roof on the ground in places. One Air-Conditioning Unit had fallen out of the wall close to where the BMW was parked. There were lengths of roof sheeting lying all over the Church yard and across the street by the Independence Park.

"Let us try to get home baby!" the wife suggested to her husband, *"I just need to see the extent of damage done to the house"* and thus began another odyssey that would last for a number of hours and leave the husband mentally drained and resigned to a fate of drowning, but it was not meant to be.

They rolled out onto Gambier Drive and slowly headed toward downtown. Their desire to navigate in that direction to get home was quickly thwarted as they noticed how much water was bogging the roadways in that direction. They turned off the road into a Church yard and spun around, moving slowly to avoid other vehicles turning around. Then they headed back past the Freeport Church out to the end of Gambier where it connected with Coral Road. They turned left and started heading up toward Express Food Store. Half-way up that road they noticed that other vehicles were turning around because of blockage caused by debris so they once again turned around and headed back down Coral Road. At the Circle the wife instructed the husband to keep left and they ventured out onto the major corridor that leads out into the rural region. A few hundred meters up this road they encountered a Tractor removing fallen trees from the roadway, but as it was clear enough to pass, they continued, until the signal was given to make a left turn off that major roadway. They had turned onto Sargeant Major road and was heading north-westerly trying to circle back into the Coral Reef neighbourhood. The water was low at first but gradually became deeper and deeper as they progressed. At one point along the roadway, after they had made at least two turns off Sargeant Major under the navigation of the wife, the water became frighteningly deep and the husband saw his life flash before his eyes. He questioned the wisdom of his dear wife, but she just told him to keep on going as she knew where they were headed. The vehicle crossed another four-way intersection in a neighbourhood unfamiliar to the husband and once again he admonished his wife to allow him to turn the vehicle around. Once again, she pointed ahead saying that it was just around a corner somewhere ahead that the worse would be and then they would be home free. The vehicle bucked and the engine sputtered, further frightening the husband especially. He now summoned all his nerves and courage and told his wife that he was refusing to go any further, asking her if she wanted them to drown out there. It was only then that she agreed and allowed him to turn the vehicle around. Silently the husband swore to never allow himself to be led by a female again against his will. They turned around and made it back approximately sixty meters, back up the way they had come when the engine finally died. The Bb was sitting in water as high as the window. Inside water was all the way up under the glove compartment which meant that the engine had been compromised. They agreed after a few frank remarks both ways, to ditch the vehicle right there and walk on home. The wife's determination to get home could have cost them their lives.

And that was how they left the vehicle and stepped out into knee-high water, stopping only to push the vehicle up onto an incline and partly onto somebody's private property. The husband was concerned about being held up because he was carrying money for his wife, now bundled into his oversized pullover. She assured him that no one would be able to tell by looking, and so they started the trek through the water trying to make it home. This journey was uneventful in terms of harm coming to them, but it was particularly nerve rending, especially for the husband who had experienced his first flooding. They meandered through trees and onto roadways identifiable by the lamp poles that marked their route. On they pushed, leaning forward to brace against the windy drizzling torrents that stung their faces and caused their clothes to stick to their skin. Lifting their knees high now, to replace their feet carefully for each stride they made, became necessary in order to allow their leg muscles to relax from constantly swinging through the wavy, heavy, salty water. They came upon the first downed electric pole and observed the power lines lying in the water. They remembered the warnings they had often heard on the radio about staying clear of downed power lines. For a moment they thought about the possibility of being electrocuted but quickly remembered that the power had been turned off hours ago. That was a voluntary sigh of relief for them both because getting home was now seeming to be an achievable reality. They got to Jack Hayward High School and pondered aloud between themselves which route to take to get home from there. Eventually they turned through a housing settlement and found themselves staring at a whole street blocked off in several places by more downed poles. The husband hesitated and wondered aloud if the power had been turned off everywhere. However they trudged on in faith mustering up the courage to venture close to a particular downed pole which provided the only point at which they could get any further along that road, and they got through, over the wires dangling in the water, between wires hanging down from the fallen poles that were supported above the ground by one obstacle or another. They had made it down one stretch of road and now discovered that there may be a shorter way home, so they turned around again and headed in a new direction, still in the general direction of home. They drifted past a house with people huddling inside and staring at them with shock and disbelief. One individual even beckoned for them to come in out of the water and driving squall. They refused, waved and smiled and kept going, until finally they saw familiar territory, still under water but so much closer to their destination. Soon they would be out of the water, at least the husband thought, but they were on wet ground in under five more minutes with the water some feet behind them. There were a few vehicles parked on the side of a small building up on an elevated plane. There were also people sitting in them, staring in disbelief at the two water-soaked individuals drifting nearer and nearer to them. They hailed, smiled and passed by. They thought they saw somebody they recognized and called him by name in passing. In another five minutes they were turning off the road in front of the blue topped Church, Central Baptist and walking up to the front of their house. To their surprise the water had receded quite a bit and they were able to see the small front porch and the lowest part of the front door. This gave them great hope and they waded a little faster into the yard. The street in the neighbourhood was as void of life as it had been when they abandoned their home a day ago and so they opened the door and slop, slopped inside. The house was a large container of water but now with a bigger leak as the water slowly flowed back out. Every few minutes it became more evident that the liquid invader was leaving and that brought a kind of joy and deepened hope. The couple glanced at each other and then went to work, picking up the shoes which were seen floating around and using broom and mop to help the water on its way out. They ventured into the kitchen and opened that side door, further increasing the volume of the drain-off. Within thirty minutes they were drying out the Bathroom and standing up the beds, having to throw water-soaked items out in the backyard in the process. Still wet and dirty, they were feeling exuberant about the chores they were doing, working like a real two-member professional team.

It was a sad day, but it was a happy one because their lives had been spared and their house had only been flooded up to twelve inches high throughout. Yes, all the items and walls that got soaked would have to be removed eventually, but for now they were still covered by its roof and enclosed by its walls. It was time for the first sip of Cup Noodles, and they had it with pleasure, sitting in one of the chairs in the living room. What happened next, and then for the remaining hours of that first day after the catastrophe, comprised mostly of cleaning up around the house, until that moment in the afternoon when the wife expressed her desire to get to her Shop. Again, and all within twelve hours, the husband found himself agreeing with her and throwing his support behind her desire. They set out from the house and trudged through the receding water along

Pioneer Way, across Coral road, heading downtown. They passed broken down trucks and buses, and curious survivors in groups who stared them down without appearing to be curious about them. The husband still carried the money his wife had given him to hold for her as they went along, avoiding the gazing eyes. Sometimes they walked alongside each other, other times there were several meters between them, but they were together, wading on. They got to the old dilapidated 'pink building' that formerly housed the Dyer Ward and other Government offices and got to the GB Power building on the right and KFC on the left. Surprisingly, after all the hours that had passed, the water was still above knee height and quite unsettled as if it was coming from several different directions to meet in this area. Mall Drive was still under unruly sea water as they pushed their way across it and turned down the right side passing the unfinished CIBC building and heading in the direction of Common-wealth Bank. Geneva's Place was before them and Culmerville Plaza was to their right. They walked across the grass and got to the rear of the little Plaza in which her Shop, Da Tuck Shop, was situated. There was no water there but more than enough evidence that there had been. They walked around the front onto McKenzie street and entered the deserted premises, looking over their shoulders for any would-be criminal-minded individuals that may be lurking around.

They let themselves into the Shop and locked the door. Cases of Soap, Body Wash containers, and a variety of Pies floated toward the briefly opened door and banked up against themselves in the little water that was left inside the building. They stopped and looked around to take it all in, destruction, loss of property, extensive damage to goods. It was all there wherever they looked but they remained calm and began the cleaning up as they had done at home.

The monster had left after slowing down to one mile per hour as it crossed Grand Bahama island. This slow movement was obviously what caused the King Tide phenomenon that pushed all that water onto the island, but now it was gone, and Bahamians breathe a sigh of relief. The process of recovery was beginning. People started assessing the extent of their loss. They began to assess what their immediate needs were, such as Gasolene for their cars, the ones that could still be driven, and so suddenly long lines appeared at all the Gas Stations and long waiting periods as individuals tried to make sure their personal needs were attended to by hogging the line with their several bottles. Some folks brought multiple family members to the line simultaneously with bottles, making it hard for the scarce commodity to be fairly distributed at the sales pump. Gasolene aside, the Food Stores had been devastated and this brought with it a shortage of food on the island. Wendy's, Burger King, Kentucky Fried Chicken, Subway, and whichever other such stores operated on the island, made a killing, some hiking the price on their fast food menu.

The people needed food, and many needed a place to shelter, so Christ the King Chapel and many others became shelters like the Freeport Seventh Day Adventist Church had become for that night of the hurricane. The difference being, Christ the King and the other churches continued as shelters long after the passage of the hurricane.

A Zombie-like state would best describe the condition of the Bahamian people during this period of the aftermath of Dorian. Curious individuals drifted about the streets of the city, looking for what only God knows, and some found it in piles of refuse, inside abandoned buildings and on private properties. These people milled around wherever there was a shipment of food supplies or an open, inviting door. They had backpacks and wore multiple suits of clothing; evidence of what they had been able to salvage from their former residence. Crosses of two colours were highly visible among the foreign NGOs and they served with diligence and love all over the island. One large distribution centre was the Independence Park where seven 40 feet long Trailers were seen being unloaded and supplies shared with the people. At the wide open area across from Rolle's Furniture Store and right by the Stoplight was another distribution point and countless persons gathered there daily to secure whatever they could for themselves and their loved ones who could not be there as a result of physical disability or illegal status. Other popular distribution centres included the 'YWCA' or the 'Y' as it is called.

God had been merciful, and the roadways had been spared, as was many of the Light poles, when the scenario is compared to hurricane Matthew of a few years earlier.

Another reality the people had to face was the absence of refrigeration, wifi, electricity, ice, and running water from their Taps. As a result, people had to be up before

8:00 to join the line at CORAL SPRINGS along Queens Highway in order to get a hold of even a single bag of ice which cost $3.00. Aliv created all kinds of Data packages to meet the growing demand for reaching out and staying in touch via wifi. The Gas Stations had lengthy lines stretching in excess of a quarter of a mile from the pumps.

Then came a loud horn one day and people looked out their windows and doors to see trailers driving slowly along the road laden with water and an assortment of food items. Uniformed persons were on board and invited people to come and get stuff for their homes. NGOs from all over the world started pouring into the Bahamas with personnel to assist with the recovery process and to distribute much needed food. It was a manifold blessing directly from God's throne and the spirit of the islanders were lifted

BTC became ALIV in a manner of speaking as Bahamians on Grand Bahama cussed out BTC and swore their undying affection to the latter. They were switching like crazy, either by number portability or the purchasing of a cheap Alcatel phone from ALIV because BTC had dropped the ball figuratively and was made to pay dearly for doing so. More lines, in rain and sun, during the week and on the Sabbath day, even dedicated Christians were spotted toeing lines because communication with the outside world had been effectively cut off. Relatives and loved ones in foreign countries had no way of knowing whether their relative residing in the country had been spared. This feeling of isolation was a thick blanket over everybody as BTC shed tears of regret and ALIV smiled on their way to the Bank…

Yes, Dorian came, and it did the two Bahamian islands right in. Thank God for NGO's wherever they came from. The outpouring of love, genuine, unselfish love was out of this world in magnitude. I don't know what the future holds, whether there will be other Dorians, or even more catastrophic hurricanes to be experienced, but one thing is certain, Dorian will never be forgotten. Not the way it battered Abaco, and then Grand Bahama; how it pushed all of the sea on land and washed away countless Haitians who were residing in the Mud on Abaco; how the frothing waters threw boats of all sizes wherever they pleased; how the monster hurricane with its strongest wind gusts somehow spared the many road surfaces and the utility poles, but in the process left

Bahamians with numerous stories of gallantry and survival, and ohhh, I could go on and on and on, but I will stop here. When you get to visit the Bahamas, pull up a chair some place, and ask anybody, what they know about Dorian. They will tell you. Just as the old wrinkled man Dorian had warned them about the possibility of flooding, in the event that, the great stone in the riverbed upslope were to become loose and roll down the river from where it had blocked its flow for many years. They will tell you about the day when that stone became unstuck and began its stampede down river and up over a low bank, in similar fashion to what was witnessed during and in the aftermath of hurricane Dorian. Ask somebody.

JAMAICAN LONG JOHN

By: Sez Hoo

I call him Long John for more than one reason. One of
the reasons was his height, bordering on seven feet.
Another reason was his way with women all over the
place, and a third reason was his love of what was right
and legal. Others sometime refer to him as John Gottie
because of the reputation he made for himself over the
years settling issues by any means necessary. According
to Long John, *"any wrongdoing mi see a gwaan mi a
report it straight to the authorities by the time yu sey
fey!"*.

He always said if the wrong doer can catch him before
he gets to the Police, they are free to kill him, but he will

be trying. Nowadays Long John don't need to physically get to the Police Station because he has a Cellular phone, and he keeps whatsapp on his home screen.

So, John happen to be hanging out down by the Harbour one afternoon, sitting on the low wall with his legs dangling inches above the water. Some men walked toward him on the wall and sat down a few meters from where he was. They were carrying on a conversation in low tones, and Long John could hear phrases like *'the stash'* and *'nuff weed'* and *'boat coming'* and *'with the white lady'* and *'tell the boss'*. Long John's ears zoned in some more and he listened intently to what they were discussing. Eventually one of them suggested that they go and get some food to eat as they had not eaten since returning to land. They got up and walked away. As soon as they were gone a hundred meters or so away, Long John whipped out his Samsung and opened whatsapp.

"Missa Adams, he texted, "mi ave a live link fi yu inna di day ya boss, link up lata ova so, yu know whey mi a talk"

Then Long John closed whatsapp and opened his Notepad app. In this app he typed in details of what he had overheard. Then he got up and walked along the edge of the wall until he got up to the Police Headquarters on Ocean Boulevard. There he crossed the road and headed up Queen street toward the heart of downtown Kingston. The Police officers knew him as a man from Jones Town who always hangs out on the waterfront begging or offering himself as help for people in need of transporting heavy loads up to where they would catch a bus home. Most days he pushed a Hand

Cart that he had made himself but today he did not have his Cart. He did however have his long barrelled .45 Magnum in his waistband under his loose- fitting shirt. He pulled on a ganga spliff as he made his way up to Parade. Yes, Long John was known but the Police did not know about his gun nor his connections to Law enforcement because the person he had texted was not stationed there.

As he walked, he surveyed the area to see whether the guys from the sea wall were anywhere in sight. He spotted them sitting on an open Terrace outside a Fast Food outlet, eating Patties and drinking Jamaican Sorrel. They were a great distance away and would not recognize him as he walked by on the sidewalk and that was that for now, and even if they did, they really did not know who he was or how he could impact their lives and operations.

As Long John walked away from Adams SUV later that evening after divulging all he had overheard downtown, he spotted a car idling down the road from where he was supposed to turn into his lane. From sixty meters away it appeared normal to see a vehicle parked where the car was. However, he was not taking any chances and so he measured the temperature of the situation by quickly rushing across to the opposite side of the road. As he did so the white Maxima sped off down the street, its tires making the hasty departure a noisy one. Long John had his Magnum in his hand and was ready for any surprises from the rogue vehicle, but none came. He quickly masked the weapon in the waist of his Jeans and pulled his shirt down. He then reached for his phone and sent a brief but terse voice message:

"Boss yu know sey some bwai jus dey ya so a program wi". *"Mi spot dem an move cross di road an di fucka dem speed off, a wah a gwaan bouya?!"* he queried into the phone as he turned into his Lane.

"Anyway nuh watch nutten, mi hav di Licence numba and description fi da cyar deh, inna mi phone. Nuh sey nutten boss!" He hung up and dropped the phone in his pocket.

The informer is never loved by those who have things to hide. He will be a target for a killing as soon as he is discovered. In my country the informer plays a very important role. There is 911 for him to call, or Crime

Stop, and today there may be newer acronyms associated to crime fighting.

The question needs to be asked though; why does the informer go out of his way to report wrongdoing in the society? Is it that he has a death wish? Does this person want to die?

I see the informer as an individual who sees the bigger picture. He can see the way things are most likely to turn out based on the things that are happening at any point in time, and so he decides out of a heart of goodness, to make an effort to put a stop to it.

Usually this is by going to the authorities and making a report. Such an individual understands what is right and what is wrong in the realm of human existence.

The reputation established over decades of experience dictates that more likely than not, something shady will be going on somewhere in Tivoli Gardens, in Jones Town, in August Town, in Wareika Hills, in Brook Valley, in Water House, in Tower Isle (tower hill), in Waltham, in Maxfield and so on, and these areas are all in Kingston. Drugs move. Guns are sold. People get high and sometimes die in these places. Informers and traitors alike, whether PNP or JLP, are disciplined. Hungry folks are fed to cement their allegiance to the goings on and to secure their lives by turning blind eyes to these goings on. These underprivileged people watch the society around them evolve from thugs riding Honda 50s to late model cars with dark tints while their standard of living remains basically maintained but unimproved.

It is into one of these depressed neighbourhoods that a white Maxima turned, out of traffic and cruised slowly along the main entrance thoroughfare to stop alongside a wall on which a group of men were lounging, chatting, chilling. They knew the car and so everyone remained in their place until it came to a stop. The driver rolled down his window and signalled to a particular man, dressed in a pair of ankle high yellow Timberlands and a thick suit more befitting for winter months. The man wore sunglasses, but had it propped on top of the cap he was wearing askance on his head. He jumped down and leaned onto the window briefly, exchanging words with the driver. Then he straightened up,

"awright boss, nuh sey a word".

He turned back to the wall as the window rolled up and the white car drove away. The other men had remained immobile on the wall, barely nodding at the car as it quietly slipped away further into the community.

These guys represent the first line of defence for this neighbourhood. Getting further in require that the visitor be interrogated by this crew and be found qualified to proceed. To the neighbourhood folks however they were just the young men from the area who refuse to go find themselves jobs and just rather to hang out every day on the wall chatting nonsense and smoking weed. How far from the truth can a person get?

What makes an army like this less than impregnable and a formidable force to deal with are the inner tensions that exists, as is played out in the following scenario:

John Paul pulled his hoodie over his head and adjusted his glasses as he strode down one of the narrow streets in his community. He made a turn onto another street and then placed his weight against a zinc fence to open a camouflaged gate in it. Then he disappeared into the yard. As far as John Paul was concerned, Blacks was scheduled to remain on watch shift, holding down the entrance to the community until midnight tonight, and his sexy girlfriend would be alone at home, waiting for him, her secret lover to arrive. When he tapped on the wooden door he was in for a big surprise.

"A who dat?!" Blacks voice rang through the otherwise quiet evening. John Paul spun around and rushed back toward the gate but not before the front door was thrown open and his crony Blacks was outlined in the opening staring at him as he fled.

"Hey bway John Paul, whe' ya' do inna man yaad fool?!"

"Mi owe yu bredda, a whe' di bumbo claat a gwaan

ya?!" Hey g'yal Janet, a wha' yu an John Paul inna?!"

As John Paul disappeared through the gate Blacks turned

back into the house and slammed the door.

Blacks draped his girlfriend as she walked into the living

room from the kitchen with his dinner. He slapped her

hard on the side of her face and pushed her against the

wall.

"A wha' mi do now baby?!" Janet hoped against hope

that he would not carry on too long with the questions,

nor beating her up. This had happened before, and she

knew him well.

Blacks stood frowning at her. She braced against the

wall with her hands held up protectively in anticipation

of swings to her face. His hands did not move.

"Cho, anyway, yu see da bway dey, mi an him a go have big things bout dis, trus' mi, him all lucky sey mi neva have mi tings pon mi dis evenin' ya!"

Blacks pulled out a chair and slumped down to have his dinner. Slowly Janet joined him at the table.

The following day was his off day and Blacks got dressed and headed out, leaving Janet gently applying a warm towel to one side of her face where he had slapped her a few times the previous evening. He caught a bus up to Papine where he visited with a few of his thug friends from that area. While there he purchased some bullets and stashed them somewhere in the thick jacket he wore. Blacks like the others in the crew, know that they cannot use the guns they are given to guard the border, for their personal business.

John Paul did not turn up for work at the entrance for a few days following that close encounter with his crony. Blacks showed but was very pensive, smoking one spliff after another and refusing to share when others needed to have a puff.

A few days later the body of John Paul was discovered in a gully he frequented on his way to and from the little board house he lived in with his baby mother Millicent, and their small son.

Another situation that weakens the gang is the illicit removal of weapons from store and failure to return it. Well such is life inside the fraternity of national rebels and their loyalists.

As they trip over each other the Police, with men like Top Cop fail to miss a beat in their efforts to bring their activities to a halt, and these cops rely on people like Long John. Top Cop leaned against his Rat Patrol Jeep and inspected the .45 pistol Long John had just handed him. He checked the safety and firing mechanisms. Then he reached into the vehicle and handed a small brown paper bag to Long John along with the weapon. The street was deserted along Old Hope Road as it was Sunday and Kingston residents are a little late in waking up. The other four Police vehicles, each with four heavily armed, blue clad men aboard, were idling along the road waiting for the exchange to be completed. Top Cop raised himself up off the vehicle and slapped Long John on his shoulder before climbing in and speeding off up the slope toward Mona. The entourage followed in similar fashion, leaving Long John by himself. He quickly jumped into his little Honda *Fit* and left the scene as well. The rendezvous had been aptly chosen, rendering their actions observable only by a person on a roof far away viewing through binoculars.

In the small rural district of Chudleigh, in the Parish of Manchester one family had relatives visiting. A young woman in her early twenties, nursing a small infant could be seen sitting on the veranda staring into space on occasions. She was John Paul's girl friend who would have to raise her son without his father now because of her illicit relationship with his thug associate known as Blacks. She knew and was planning to get even in time. Of course, her getting even would more than likely have to involve the boss of the neighbourhood enforcers, and could result in Blacks losing his life, or her losing hers and that of her young son, depending on how the boss viewed the situation. For the time being Patsy, as her name was, is content with being away from the inner-city community and away from any further actions by Blacks or his cronies in keeping with Gang codes and norms. For now, her relatives and the members of this community would have to simply accept her and do the best they can to help her re-integrate.

The daily routine at the entrance to the community mentioned earlier, continued as usual but with one man short. The White Maxima came and went, and messages were dropped and picked up. As they carried out their drug running and Arms distribution business they were on the lookout for the tall skinny man who had been spotted in an uptown neighbourhood chatting candidly with known renegade top brass cops; the same man who had whipped out a .45 Magnum upon seeing the car and had caused them to beat a hasty retreat from the area.

This man was not known to any of them and it puzzled them big time.

At the same time, no one ever saw the real boss, even though most persons had a fair idea who he was. Where he lived, now that was a big secret. All messages dropped and picked up from the entrance came with his permission and the responses went back to him wherever he happened to be.

Long John went about his daily life as the average Jamaican does. He is a father, a married man, with siblings. He had a home and went to work every day, downtown on the Harbour where he operates as a Franchise holder of a small mobile business. Long John kept his eyes open for activities along the waterfront and had recently discovered the likely arrival of drugs and weapons to the island. He had done his part by reporting

it to his connections in the Police Force and had been
rewarded with a fresh supply of ammunition for his
Magnum. He was strutting with that confidence
downtown again when he spotted the Maxima as the
occupants spotted him. Time stopped long enough for
him to ease the long-barrelled Magnum from his
waistband and depress its trigger. He did it quicker and
the white car felt its impact in four places in an instant.
Then Long John sprinted up King Street concealing the
big gun as he went. After running for a few seconds and
blending into the crowd busy shopping, he slowed to a
walk and continued to make his way up the sidewalk,
past Policemen doing foot patrol in the area. They had
no idea. He was just another person going about his
business. Down the street the white Maxima had taken
fire and as it turned out, three of the four occupants had

been hit and three of them fatally. When the Policemen swarmed the scene from all over the downtown area, the driver was slouched on the vehicle staring into its darkened interior and swearing loudly. Some of the responding officers fisted their handguns and had them aimed at the distraught man. Inside the car three men were bleeding to death from holes in their heads. Each man was clutching a handgun and there were two high-powered rifles laying on the floor. People had gathered like ravens to inspect the spoils of what they understood to be the on-going drug war in the city.

One senior Officer made his way through the crowd and took a brief look inside the car. He straightened himself up and spoke into his radio:

"Let me confirm the shooting incident along King Street. It is now 8: 43 A.M., Tuesday…Three men are still in a

white Maxima motorcar with gunshot wounds to their heads. We have in our custody a fourth man whom we saw at the scene, standing over a Glock pistol. He did not resist the Police. There is no sign of the shooter. Some people on the scene are confessing that everything happened in a blur and it is hard to describe. One man remembers seeing a tall man running away from the scene with a gun in his hand, heading up King Street. That's it for now". The radio screeched and sputtered then became silent as the officer hung it back onto his shiny black belt.

Top Cop rested his hand akimbo and scanned the crowd, letting his gaze settle on one of the officers who accompanied him to the scene.

"This is war squaddie, yu recognize dem man dey inna di cyar?" he pointed with his chin toward the car.

He then took out his cell phone and dialled a number, stepping away from the officer as he did so.

"Boss di man dem spot mi an right awey dem brakes up, roll dung window an a bare guns mi see a rise up through di window dem. As a soldier yu know sey mi always strap so mi pop off and it look like mi beat dem, a dat gwaan".

"Asi, so dat a cum from di odda day when dem si me an yu a reason up so, okay, so it illegal fi a citizen talk with the Police then, awright, stay safe" the Khaki uniformed Officer ended the telephone conversation. He turned around and stepped back over to where the other Policemen had the man from the shot-up car restrained.

As time passed the five years that spanned between General Elections gradually slipped away. Unlike former years, when diehard, loyal supporters of either National Political Parties would get on Band Wagons and drive around in Party colours, chanting the name of their charismatic leader and songs they had been taught by the creative minds in the hierarchy of the Party; no, these days the approaching of a General Election stirred the passion of a minority, made up most likely of people who did not know enough about either of the parties, or about what really goes on in Jamaican politics. These days people focused on making money, by legal and illicit means. The concern of many such individuals was to make sure that the arena in which they make their money is kept free of informers, like Long John. Long John on the other hand, know he needed to stay extremely alert and wily, to stay alive. He did not sleep in the same place twice. He also made sure that his supply of ammunition never dwindled. Long John had close friends everywhere who knew him as a Gunman, but none of them knew him as an informer.

After the shooting Downtown in which a white Maxima was shot up and three men died, Long John took away himself from Kingston. The Saturday night following that incident found him attending a Dance in south Trelawny, in a little district named Wait-A-Bit. Some guys from the area, fresh back from Farm work in America had promoted the Dance. While chilling with a few friends there, absorbing bass and storing lyrical content in his brain, in the late hours of the night, a entourage of the Jamaica Labour Party rolled onto the scene, blaring horns and chanting, as outdated as the practice had become. Men jumped from the backs of trucks and quickly mingled with the patrons, some of whom were thronging the sides of the road in the vicinity

of the Dancehall in which BLACK CAT, the heavy

weight Sound was blasting. The roadway was the only

one through the area and the Dance created an epicentre

for the night. People were in attendance from as far away

as Troy and Christiana to check out their favourite

Sound and Selector, Panther.

By a stroke of luck, or providence, Long John barely

caught a glimpse of a familiar face and dropped the spliff

he had been sucking on, allowing himself the excuse to

bend down in order to retrieve it. As he did there was a

single explosion and a flash of light streaked across the

darkness in his direction. His friends had also been wary

and had imitated his ducking motion before asking him

why he did it. The bullet missed them and by the time

the other multiple explosions came, they had removed

themselves and were mingling in the crowd of writhing bodies all over the roadway. Long John by then had his Magnum in his fist but held close to his torso, moving at three quarters of his height and swivelling around every few seconds to scan his surroundings.

John Paul deserted his friends in the crowd and made his way a few hundred meters down the road in the darkness to where he had parked his car in somebody's yard when he first arrived. As he slumped down into the seat his mind raced, *"How di bloodclaat dem bway ya know sey mi dey a country, mi bumbo claat!"*

Long John started the engine and then got on his Cell phone.

"Yow bredda, mi a leggo bou'ya fi right now seen. Link up lata, mi wi call di I seen, bless up!" On the other end

of the line his breddren responded, *"Nuh watch nutten John, we a go fine out a who dem bway dey an mek yu know, yu done know!"*

With that being done he slowly eased the Honda *Fit* out of the yard and started his withdrawal from the frontline.

Back at the Dance the Labourites had applauded the sudden bursts of gunfire, thinking it was another of the usual indications by a firearm holder to request that the Selector play the song being played, a second time. In the narrative of the Dancehall, *"Pull up Selecta!!!"*

Black Panther the selector had shouted into the Microphone at the time, *"LEEEGGGAALLL!!!* and had immediately lifted the needle from the vinyl 45 Record and replaced it at the beginning to start the Dub Plate over. Now, five minutes later everyone had settled back into doing what they had been doing before the shots were heard; bubbling and wining, and sipping drinks, the cheaper ones from dark bottles while the extravagant ones sipped from crystal glasses whatever they pour from the tall bottles they had resting on party tables near to their spot. The costumes were as extravagant as the price of some of the drinks they sipped, and the Dance continued. Through the crowd small boys moved around collecting bottles and stacking them in crates as a favour to the Promoter. They would be rewarded for doing so after the Dance was over. The Jerkman, the Soupman and the other vendors were all busy making their money as patrons thronged around their stalls eagerly waiting on their orders to be completed and served. Long John's cronies kept their distance and their hands wrapped around their weapons, burning spliffs and rocking to the sweet Reggae music.

It was a typical Big Dance scene as it usually is played out in Jamaica around General Elections time.

Long John did not return to Kingston. Instead he headed west in the direction of lower Trelawny, driving carefully as he navigated the winding road that traversed the mountainous terrain from Wait-A-Bit.

Elsewhere, in Chudleigh, on the Sunday morning following the Dance in Wait-A-Bit, a car pulled up at a small Shop along the roadway and the driver, the only occupant asked some boys hanging out on a rough bench outside the shop whether they knew a girl named Millicent who just moved into the area with a little baby boy. The boys looked at each other questioningly and one of them asked, *"who dat?!"*

Another boy rocked his head, *"Millicent...girl wid baby bway...jus move inna di area, oh mi know a who ya'talk, she live right up inna da Lane dey!"* he stood up and pointed as his friends stared at him in disbelief. The driver pushed out his closed fist and opened it to reveal a $1000.00 bill. The boy grabbed it and said a quick, *"Respec father, jus aks anybody inside dey fi show yu har house!"*

The car drove off and turned into the Lane.

"Yu si yu same bway Goosie, yu mouth a go get yu inna big trouble one a dem day ya, memba mi tell yu!"

Another boy chimed in, *"Eeh, yu no even know di man. Yu know him Goosie,… s'pose a cum him cum fi kill di ooman, a yu woulda cause it inno!"*

As that was happening in Chudleigh, young men were on their way to their hangout spot near the entrance to their community in Western Kingston. They chatted about the disappearance and later discovery of the body of their croney John Paul whose body had been found with gunshot wounds some time ago and about the recent shooting and killing of their boss's bodyguards in downtown Kingston a few days ago. Every one of them was frowning and tensed, wondering what was really going on. Information was sure to come to them soon, it always did.

Inside the BLACK CAT Dance in Wait-A-Bit three men leaned against one side of the Lawn burning spliffs and drinking Beers. One of them was wearing tight fitting Jeans and T Shirt. His shirt snuggled against a familiar bulging shape in his waist. The other two had long nosed high-powered weapons slung over their shoulders and were standing stock still, not talking but constantly scanning the sea of people all around them dancing. Every few seconds they would glance toward the entrance.

Near to them a member of Parliament was sitting on a stool at a Bar with his entourage, drinking. He had instructed the Bar keeper to dole out drinks to anyone who came near and was interested. He was laughing and having a great time as the night wore on and the flashing Neon lightings painted his features and form in radiating hues every passing second.

Long John got to the intersection where a Signpost gave directions: one arrow pointing out one road which went back up into south Trelawny while another arrow pointed in another direction where a road went on through a Cane field toward Clarks Town and beyond. He stuck to the Clarks Town road and pressed gas. After driving for a few hundred meters along the lonely roadway flanked by growing sugar cane on both sides Long John spotted a narrow parochial road that led off the road into the Cane Field. He turned the car onto this road, drove a short distance in and switched off the engine and lights. This spot would be his home for this night he thought as he tilted the seat back and closed his eyes, clutching his Magnum firmly in his hand.

On Monday morning School boys on their way to Meadowbrook High School were deep in discussion about social issues facing their country.

"Kevin yu ever hear bout one badman dem call Long John?!"

The boy named Kevin shook his head, *"A who name so and whey him cum from DeMarco?"*

"Yes mi hear bout him!" another boy, Orlando, *affectionately called Lanzo,* interjected. *"Dem sey a him shot di man dem dung town las week inna di white Maxima!"*

"How him alone fi shot three man and dem have gun pon dem?!" Marco exclaimed.

"A dat mi a sey too, Kevin reacted, *'cause mi hear sey di man dem whey dead a gunman. Dem sey di Police dem fine all kinda guns inna di cyar Lanzo!"*

"Bway him brave nuh clothesline, trus'mi". "Fi one man pull off dat, him mussy really a sharp shoota!".

The boys got to the School gate and left the conversation there as they greeted the Security Guard, zipped open their backpacks for inspection, and made their way inside the Campus.

As the morning passed the thugs watching the inner-city community entrance mumbled among themselves, swearing their determination to preserve their lives despite the uncertainty that hung in the air. One of them summed it up like this:

"A one ting me know dawg, nuh bway nah cum lick off my head ova nuh ooman, or nutten else fi dat matta. Mi have a piece whey di boss gi mi an mi nuh fraid fi use it. Is all about watching yu 'ead back my youth, a dat mi sey"

"Yu mean like dis, a so yu watch yu 'ead back?" one of the others pressed his pistol against the back of the one talking and released the safety mechanism. The young thug almost jumped out of his skin.

"Whe di bumbo claat ya' deal wid Shadow, yu always up to some kinda fuckery, all when man a chat bout serious business!" *"Big and serious man, there is a time fi playing and a time fi serous reasonin', chill out man an cut out di foolishness"*. They both shoved their weapons back into their waistbands as the others had a good laugh. Shadow raised his hand, palm open for his

frightened crony to slap. Debo's scowl disappeared and he slapped palms with Shadow as they settled down to continue their tireless vigil. A few moments after a cell phone rang and the news came to them about what was going on. It was the survivor of the recent shooting downtown. He was calling from the Half Way Tree Police holding cell where he had been incarcerated and was awaiting a Court date.

"yeah, as mi a show yu, di boss soo free mi still but a no dat, yu know sey a di same tall black bredda whey wi did a spy pon whey day up so, kill di man dem?!"

"Is like wi spot him dung town an we a pree fi tun him ova but di fucka spot wi same time an ease of a ras claat ugly Magnum mi bredda. Before mi know whe a gwaan him squeeze off four and three a dem find di target inna di cyar to blood claat. Mi hear a likkle ting sey him a

work wid Police though, informer aka enforcer fi dem

right now" "Anyway lata when mi come out wi chat, mi

si di Babylon bway a cum fi run mi offa di phone, lata

yow!" The thug listening hung up the phone and dropped

it back into his pocket.

"Di I dem hear breddren…is a informa bway kill di man

dem inno. Squiddly sey di bway a wuk wid Police

though, so a dat a gwaan"

"Blood claat, mi cyaa believe sey di man dem drop out,

trus'mi!" one of them shook his head slowly.

Back in Chudleigh Manchester the car had driven only

fifty meters into the Lane when the driver slowed and

asked an elderly woman who had stepped out of the road

to allow the vehicle to pass. The lady pointed to a house

up on a slope above the road, *"the only new girl wid*

baby living here is in that yard up there sah" The driver

thanked her by handing her a $1000.00 bill and then

pulled off the road to park as she went on her way. He

came out and stood staring up at the house.

"Millicent!" he shouted, *"Millie!, Millie!...Millicent!"*

he started up the slope toward the brightly painted house,

hoping to see or hear her respond. A young lady

appeared on the veranda above and stood trying to figure

out who was calling her name so loudly. She observed

the person coming up the slope but was unable to see his

face, until he paused and called out her name again,

raising his head as he did.

"Uncle Bertie! Uncle Bertie!! Whoooaaayyy!!!" *"Is how*

yu fine mi uncle?!" She spun around and disappeared as

she made her way back through the house to get to the

stairs that led down to the ground. The man started

laughing, loudly and exclaiming, *"so a which part yu cyan go inna dis island dat mi couldn't fine yu Millicent?!"* He hurried his steps to get up to where the steps from the house stopped. His niece Millicent was already coming down the stairs, shouting his name and grinning. They crashed into each other and squeezed for a very long time without talking. They were overcome with emotions that flushed their faces.

Eventually she released her uncle and tugged his hand, *"come uncle, come up mek mi give yu a chair mek yu res yu foot so wi cyan talk"* They went up the stairs together and onto the veranda. From this altitude uncle Bertie was treated to a panoramic view of the parish as well as sections of Trelawny. He was amazed at the way the landscape was mostly covered with Yam fields and greenery. The other fascinating thing for him was the constant flow of cool air. He sat down and waited on his niece to bring him the promised drink. She came back with a tall glass and three other individuals; one middle aged woman, her husband, and a boy and introduced them to him as her late boyfriend's parents and sibling. Uncle Bertie stood up and greeted them heartily with firm handshakes and his broadest smile. Then they sat down to enjoy the lemonade, the cool breeze and the scenery, and Millicent started updating her uncle with the details that led her to visit the home of her in-laws.

"yes, so uncle Bertie mi bway frien John Paul obviously was cheatin on mi wid girls all ova di place up a town and him neva stop until him go fool roun one a him gangsta frien dem ooman an di man ketch him inna him yaad one evenin. Him get whey da evenin dey but di bway swear sey him a go kill him an him do it uncle.

"Right down inna di foot track whey him always walk when him a come een an go out him kill him. Mi sey man, when mi hear sey him dead mi couldn believe it, because mi know sey mi have him young young baby a raise an dat di baby need him fawda" Millicent wiped tears from her eyes. The baby cried out and she got up to get him from his Crib inside. Momentarily she returned carrying a chubby boy wrapped in his swaddlings and sucking her breast. The baby took one brief glance at the strange man and refocused on his feeding.

Uncle Bertie hung his head and shook it.

It is always like this in Jamaica: the boy turns rogue maybe because he was born into the world under strange twisted circumstances and disappointed early by those who were supposed to show him love. He grows up to at least ten years of age and by then decides that he is going to have to fend for himself if he is to survive. His decision is reinforced by realities around him, including the beckoning of personalities in the criminal underworld. The average boy falls into the web because in the web he makes money to take care of himself, but he makes the money by involving himself in illegal activities, which often exposes him to real danger on occasions. The boy once in the web, hardly ever gets out of it with his life. There is always something that messes him up, be it a fallout with the boss; a disagreement between him and another lost youngster; unfair practices involving money; confrontation with the Police; confrontation with members of other Gangs, and the list can go on. Whichever way it happens, the boy usually comes out the loser. Then the fallout from his death is the baby mother left to raise his child or children. There is his family and the family of the baby mother, left to mourn and grieve the loss of their relative, as the vicious cycle continues. As is the case with John Paul, luckily for his baby mother, there is an uncle who loves her and takes the time to seek out her whereabouts; that is not always the case. Then on the other hand, the other boy, Blacks, responsible for the killing, is now in fear of being discovered as the killer, which would create a scenario in which he could be hunted and killed by the Police, or friends of the dead John Paul; reprisal after reprisal after reprisal becomes possible, ceasing only if, and when, something new and exciting overwhelms the community and takes the attention from the cycle of killing, to money making, migrating prospects, or other such things.

"So Millie what going to happen now, what kinda plans yu makin, because I don't believe you people dem goin allow yu fi jus live inna dem house permanently an jus feed yu an di likkle bway fi free like dat!"

"Uncle mi start a likkle days work wid one a di neigbors dem a'ready inno, two days outta di week mi wash clothes fi one ooman up di hill dey so and she pay mi good money, enough fi buy mi baby tings and feed mi'self"

Uncle Bertie nodded his head and a brief smile flashed across his face.

"Anyway, yu rememba sey yu fawda did a file fi yu from long time right, fi get yu ova farrin wid him?" Millicent smiled and nodded, *"Yeah, mi rememba, who wouldn' rememba something like dat?"*

"Well him tell mi di las time mi call him, sey the filing soon come through now, so mi a mek yu know sey jus' hol' on an do yu bes' ya'so until yu get the news awright?" The others sitting by were listening attentively and the two adults smiled and nodded, praising God for his goodness.

"Well Millicent, mi glad sey mi fine whey yu a stay and mi wi' come back cum look fi yu whenever mi c'yan okay" he reached into his pocket and pulled out his Wallet, from which he took a small stack of thousand dollar bills and handed them to her. Millicent hugged her uncle and thanked him with a quick smooch on his cheek. He raised himself up and stood looking out over the elevated veranda at the beautiful scenery for a few moments. The day had worn on and he could smell the

Sunday dinner being prepared inside the kitchen somewhere in the house. Uncle Bertie spoke again,

"I will keep in touch with you guys okay, mi haffi leave now 'cause mi have some odda tings fi deal wid inna di city dey today"

"Yu mean yu not staying fi dinna uncle?!"

"Maybe next time Millie, nuh feel no way, Mr. and Mrs. Paul, thanks for taking in mi niece yu hear, mi really appreciate the gesture because unoo neva haffi dweet, God bless!"

"No problem Bertie, we actually glad sey yu come look fi har man, because wi know sey she have family somewhey who mus' have love fi har, God is good mi bredda, praise Him". They shook hands and he started to leave.

"Take care uncle Bertie!" John Paul's sibling, who had been quiet all through the conversation, spoke up from where he was leaning against a column of the veranda, *"travel safe back to Kingston!"*

Uncle Bertie thumped fists with him and went past him down the stairs. The family followed him down to the road and watched him turn the car around.

"Awright Bertie, come again whenever yu feel like, jus show up awright, yu don't need to tell us ahead of time, jus come een!"

The men thumped fists and the wife waved as he started to drive away.

"Blessings!" Uncle Bertie responded.

News of the killings in downtown Kingston had spread across the island like a swift wind and now it was the main discussion, from hoodlums to churchgoers. Everybody wanted to know who this person was that had single-handedly wiped out the lieutenants of one of the most notorious gangs from West Kingston. Everybody knew that meant long term, large scale war in the country, again, as memories of illustrious gangsters like Jim Brown, and others flashed through their minds.

The guns were already out, and bounties declared on the head of the guilty party, running into millions of dollars. Already there has been shootings across borderlines where suspicion created a cloud of doubt and misgivings. A red BMW had replaced the white Maxima that had been shot up, and three new gang members had been assigned to handle city wide patrol and date management; this crew collected information on the ground and made it available to the top man while it was relevant and even before the information was too well known, just to keep him on the cutting edge of whatever went on in the underworld of criminality. In a similar way, the Police keep people like Long John armed and dangerous in exchange for the information that he provides.

Three weeks following the killing the Funeral had been arranged, and despite the heavy downpour in Saint Catherine, virtually everybody who knew anything about Kingston's inner-city culture, was in attendance. Three beautiful Caskets were mounted side by side, made even more beautiful by the load of wreaths and Cards that seemed to be everywhere around them. A sign emblazoned above the Caskets bore the inscription: "*MERCENARIES DON'T DIE: They only go to Hell to regroup*"; a statement borrowed from the writings of some classic literary enthusiast. A flamboyant Minister of the Gospel detailed the lives of the dead in beautiful poetic language as he heaped praiseworthiness upon their short lives, so richly lived, according to him. The crowd sang lustily all the songs as they were raised, totally ignoring the fact that they were being soaked by the drenching rain. While on the wider outskirts of the Cemetery those who kept watch, did so from the confines of their tinted vehicles. In the crowd Long John stood, dressed in a black suit and matching sunglasses, like all the other men there and sung along like someone who really loved and cared for, and was truly mourning the untimely passing of the three dead thugs. Informers rarely ever know the identity of other informers, and especially if they were also enforcers for the Constabulary and so Long John had to blend in as effectively as he could so he could pick up whatever information he could from this Funeral

gathering. He moved when the crowd moved, never

against the wave of motion. He kept his glasses on just in

case the gathering was being scoped by high powered

lenses from a distance, and he made sure to keep his face

turned toward the Caskets. Elsewhere in the crowd top

Cop and a few of his dedicated entourage of officers

moved freely, clad in black suits and ties as well. Every

man strapped, as tightly as Long John was. The showers

ceased and the sermon ended. The three Caskets were

being lowered into the concrete cavern, one on top of the

other. Two men were removing the suspended

inscription from where it had been mounted above the

Casket display area, when the shooter from Wait-A-Bit

caught the attention of Long John. He had removed his

sunglasses only briefly to wipe his eyes. Long John

studied him carefully and discovered that he was in the company of another armed individual. As the procession drifted back to their vehicles, he slowed his stride a little. His first bullet passed went through the skull of the Wait-A-Bit shooter and toppled him backwards onto his friend. There was no sound and it appeared as if the man had fainted. His friend caught his sagging body and started to lay him down when he noticed the gaping hole in his forehead. He dropped the dying body and tried to reach under his Louis Vitton Jacket, but his hand didn't make it there. A second round of high velocity hot metal knocked a cylindrical hole in his right knee and extracted a trail of bone and ligament which splashed onto the fabrics of people passing by, as his body buckled and was flung backwards. Still no sound, but the two passers-by started screaming as they noticed the blood oozing from the hole in the head of one man, and knee of the other man now laying prostrate on the wet grass. This initial scream caused the crowd to panic and everyone started running as fast as they could toward their vehicles. Top Cop and his squaddies had been alerted by the sudden commotion and each man now had his side piece gripped firmly as they swivelled around the bodied of rushing people in an attempt to spot whoever it was that had started the commotion. They had not heard any shots fired and were wondering what the commotion was about. Out on the road somebody opened-up a high-powered weapon into the sky, heightening the trepidation. Then there was a mad screaming of tires as vehicles hastily sped away from Dovecot. Long John had joined the rushing throng as soon as he had dispatched those two Wait-A-Bit goons, and was now driving along in the queue heading toward Spanish Town. The Police were the last to leave the Dovecot property and as they scoured the grounds they stumbled upon the victims. One man was obviously dead while a second man was writhing around and gripping his right knee where blood was gushing out onto bone fragments on the grass. Some sixty feet from where the bodies lay, top Cop found two spent shells and quickly pocketed them.

"Alright guys, I have called the relevant authorities and they are on their way here as we speak to secure these bodies". "I can also safely tell you guys that this shooting was not a random act". "I will be expecting to hear from Long John soon regarding this"

As the Funeral queue made its way along the wet road back toward Spanish Town, a Honda *Fit,* part of the procession, slowed and pulled out onto a small narrow side Lane. The driver switched off the engine and sat waiting for the long line of vehicles to pass. It was noisy as several SUVs had music blaring from their open windows in a show of solidarity for those left behind at Dovecot.

In their collective psyche the war would continue, and another set of individuals would soon accompany the corpses of their loved ones to this very place, whether it be Lawyer, Doctor, or Indian Chief.

Later that same evening, long after the Funeral had ended and the crowd had dispersed, and night had fallen over the parish of Saint Catherine; after Long John had smoked several Cigarettes and downed a half a dozen bottles of Heineken at a Bar in the Lane, right off the main road, he got into the small car and backed out onto the road. With his taillights toward Spanish Town he drove away from that scene, with one intention in mind.

After meandering along the narrow roadway that led into the hinterlands of the parish Long John turned off the road onto the Dovecot property and doused his lights. Looking around cautiously to see if he was being watched, he walked to the back of the vehicle and removed a Sledgehammer, a Cold forged Chisel, and a Crowbar. He dropped them into a backpack and quietly closed the rear door down. Then the darkness enveloped his already dark form. In the dark he carefully made his way, going by memory, back to the recent burial Tile. Once there he pried the newly installed concrete covering slab loose and began robbing the Casket. He went to the second and the third and did the same; removing any, and all valuables that were buried with the dead. Then he replaced the slabs of concrete and retraced his steps to his car. No one had seen him as everybody had retired to their premises after the rain and the Funeral, and most of the attendees were from Kingston and had headed back home directly anyway.

As he sat in the car, before starting the engine Long John made the sign of the cross across his forehead and upper body and began inspecting the items he had retrieved. There were three brand new Rolex watches, three diamond rings, three thick, golden bracelets, and three wads of U.S. dollars which he counted and realized that he had made himself three thousand dollars richer in American currency. Long John was excited about the haul. He took one last glance, peering out into the darkness before starting the engine and creeping away.

Will the night creatures tell what they have witnessed? Probably not.

Before long, no more than a week after the shooting at the Funeral, the leaders of the gangs in West Kingston called a truce and a meeting was arranged to take place inside the old Majestic Cinema. The spot was isolated and apart from the faded sign, quite nondescript to the passing eye. Men were instructed to unlock the large gate that barred the entrance since its closure decades ago, and the vehicles rolled in at random times in keeping with the schedule start time. At the end of that meeting it was agreed that all gangs would work together to get rid of this anonymous persona non grata that had been wreaking havoc in recent months. Plans were put in place, inclusive of the assistance of Police personnel who made money on the side by supporting gang activities. Money was distributed and everybody left the meeting totally re-dedicated and hyped up about the situation at hand. Their problem however was, they didn't even have a name or a picture, nothing to work with…so far.

At home in Mona Heights Long John slept like he hadn't done in a long time. Maybe he was comforted by the influx of money he retrieved from those corpses at Dovecot, and those Jewellery items he would be selling soon. Now his household could be taken care of in the manner he had long dreamt of. He slept so deeply that he snored and didn't come awake. The Lane in which he lived had a peaceful, residential, comfortable feel to it, kind of homely put another way. His wife knew that he worked in tandem with the Police on serious cases, as he had shared with her. She did not know that he was really a renegade with a gun who shot people in the process of keeping the streets safe for the average person to traverse as they sought to earn their livelihood. She lay with him and slept, not in the least bothered by his snoring. She saw him as a great provider, and she loved him dearly. His children loved him just as much as their mother and showed him by their hugs every chance they got. When daddy slept like this they thought, he must be truly tired, and so they allowed him to sleep. Long John slept all through that day following the Funeral at Dovecot, only awaking in time for his dinner at approximately 5:30 p.m.

Weeks later, on a day when Millicent was out shopping for new baby clothes, and thugs were out in numbers all over the corporate area, when the Police were busy battling warring factions who dared to confront them; on a day when drugs were being distributed from Park benches and community entrance hangout spots across Jamaica, Long John thought it safe to drive all the way to Montego Bay to pawn the Rolexes and other Jewellery. He arrived there mid-morning, after the business places were all up and running, and approached the most exquisite looking Pawn Shop he could find in the city.

"Mornin' boss man. I have a few items here that I would love to pawn or sell directly to you this mornin" he spoke through the ceiling high glass barricade to the middle-aged gentleman standing there with both hands pressed firmly against the glass topped counter.

"Sure, what yu got there, let me see" his eyes gleamed.

Long John reached in and pulled out one of the Rolexes and rested it on the counter where the glass had stopped

8 or so inches from touching the counter. The man

picked up the watch and his one eyed binocular and

began staring closely at the watch through it. After a full

minute of scrutinizing the watch he rested it down on the

counter and asked, *"Are you selling it to me, or pawning*

it to return for it?"

"Actually I have two other just like that one, here, take a

look at them"

The Store owner looked past Long John out the door and

responded, *"Give me one second, let me close this door*

an give us a bit more privacy if you don't mind, that's

okay with you sir?"

Long John glanced around, weighing the suggestion in

his mind briefly, and then agreed. The man pressed a

button concealed under the counter, and the shutter

slowly rolled down until it was a mere foot from the pavement.

"Okay, let's do business my good man" he took up one watch after the other and inspected them as he did the first. Then he held up his head and said, *"How much do you want for the lot?"*

Long John counteracted, *"I am here primarily to ask you to tell me the price for these items sir. Then and only then will I be able to make a decision to sell or not".*

"Okay, let me see", he pulled out a Magazine and opened it to display pictures of all kinds of watches, *"let's see, let's see, okay, watches like these are worth US$40,000 to US$50,000 a piece so for the three you are looking at anywhere from US$140,000 to US$150,000*

right here sir" he smiled at Long John and fidgeted a little.

"Okay, how about...never mind boss" *"I would love to sell you those three watches right now"* *"Here is my Banking information, you may deposit the funds there right away and these fine Rolex watches are yours to keep"* Long John smiled for the first time. The gentleman reached for the strip of paper he had handed to him, and typed the information into his gadget. Then he typed in US$150,000 and pressed *'SEND'*

"Okay, there you are sir, the money is in your account. It was a real pleasure doing business with you" He handed back the strip of paper to Long John and pressed the button to raise the store front shutter.

"Okay, one last thing for me to do here and that is to verify that the funds are actually there in my account, allow me to make an enquiry of my own please"

"Don't worry, you should be receiving a message just about now, telling you that your account have been credited the sum we discussed okay. At that same moment Long John's cellular phone lit up and the small digital voice came through, *'message received'*. The message confirmed the deposit and he walked out of the Store. As he walked out the hard metal handle of his long-nosed Magnum knocked against the vertical runner of the shutter and brought the Store owners' attention to focus on the large before seen bulge under Long John's shirt. In a moment Long John was gone. He had parked his car a safe distance away and he made his way there now as quickly as he could. As soon as he drove away

from where he had parked the idea came to him to make

a withdrawal and he pulled into the first Banking

Complex he came upon. Inside the ABM he slid his Card

in and selected US Dollars. Then he selected Withdrawal

and punched in 20,000 to test the system. The machine

churned out the US$20,000.00 and he pocketed the cash.

At the next stop he made Long John walked into a Store

and bought himself a new suit. He dressed right there

and walked out, dapper as they come. Next, he stopped

at another Bank and introduced himself as an investor.

He then requested that his money be transferred from the

account it had been placed on, onto three other separate

accounts, all in his name. He explained when prompted,

that he is about to make payments to his US clients but

they needed to be able to access their funds and the

accounts they have access to are the ones he is

requesting that the funds be transferred into. The Bank complied with the request, having seen nothing wrong with the accounts and Long John thanked them and left.

At the Pawn Shop the Store owner was still pondering over his good fortune. He knew he would be making a huge profit from those three Rolexes since the Magazine he had opened only showed last years prices. Those watches were now being sold for close to US$80,000.00 each. He smiled to himself as he swabbed them and placed them in the display tray inside the thick glass showcase.

Long John made it back to Kingston safely and without incident that evening and surprised everybody in his household with his new dapper appearance.

"My family, my loved ones, guess what, things are about to change, and big time too!" he chuckled as he sat down to rest his legs in the small Living room. His wife and children came close and crammed themselves into the long settee beside him. At that moment his phone rang and he got up. *"Yow, a who dis?!",* he rasped into the instrument. *" Biggs, what a gwaan hills man, bway from mi lef out dung a di Dance mi not even link di I eeh, is a shame, sorry bout dat mi breddren, wha' a gwaan diff'rently?"*

The conversation went on until Long John finally said, *"hear wha' a gwaan, text mi yu account numba mek mi drop some money in dey fi di I later this week, seen, mi eat a likkle food an mi wa'an di I enjoy some a it"*

... *"awright bless up, lata hills man!"* He hung up and returned to sit with his family. As he sat down he got back up, *"I just rememba sumting, mek mi mek da quick call ya an den mi cum back an continue wha' mi did a sey, please okay!"* He walked away into the bedroom.

"Top Cop, long time, how tings goin' wid you an the Team?"

"Lissen, the man dem who get shot ova Dovecot a me shot dem boss. Couple weeks ago mi dung a Wait-A-Bit a one Dance and the one wid di damaged knee clap up some shot afta mi and some a mi breddren dem without a cause boss. Dem come on a di Dance with a entourage a JLP supporters and jus' open up pon wi inna di big crowd mi a talk inno. Is a good ting sey man well trained an mi spot dem from dem jump offa di truck back boss. If we neva duck a dead body dem woulda pick up, trus' mi!". *"Anyway, apart from dat, anodda big shipment a drugs and guns a cum een tomorrow dung inna Sainty,*

somewhey inna di swampy area dung dey. Dis one ya big

so mek sure sey unoo properly strapped an equipped fi

hangle big shit. Accordn to wha' mi hear, is a big crew

from Mexico and Guatemala a hangle the front so be

careful, carry the whole crew wid yu seen. Mi pick dat

up a di same Funeral a Dovecot, nuh watch nutten. Di

drop a anywhey between Sat'dey night an Sundey

mawnin, so get inna di place early so unoo c'yan scope

out tings propaly, blessings Top Cop. Keep in touch".

Long John returned to the Settee this time and
apologized as he sat down.

As life churned on in Jamaica the news got around that
graves at Dovecot had been robbed after a Funeral. A
certain Pawn Shop owner heard the News, but he kept
quiet as he anticipated making his hefty profit. Its life
and its fair game he thought to himself. Money has no

real friends. On the crime front three loners had been shot and killed so far across the Corporate area as thugs determined to end the life of the person responsible for their recent losses. Each victim turned out to be ordinary young men walking home from a girlfriends' place or on their way there at night. The Police now had the job of figuring out who killed those three young men and the motive behind the killings. Unfortunately for the Police, some among their ranks knew and will not tell. Top Cop and his team went to Saint Elizabeth and successfully dismantled the operations there, seizing the entire loot that was brought in; hundreds of guns of various calibers and an extremely huge stash of illegal narcotics. Following that drug bust all members of the Top Cop crew, including Top Cop himself, were promoted.

Six months later, on a warm Tuesday afternoon, Long John sat with his family waiting on his flight to New York to arrive, he listened to the News on his phone and a smile broke through his hardened features to reveal pearly white teeth, closely fitted and even in height. His wife caught that flash and returned her version of pearly whites. Their children, seated nearby, were focusing on one game or the other on their electronic gadgets.

Long John had gotten to this point after getting his Passport and US Visa renewed and then applying for and receiving Passports and Visas for his wife and children. Good-bye Jamaica and good-bye poverty he thought to himself as he sat there. It had been a long stretch, but somehow God had seen past his stern evil ways and had kept him. He had been able to successfully pawn the bracelets and rings as he had pawned the watches and had also successfully transferred the monies to his different accounts so as not to arouse suspicion by overloading a single account. He was basically a rich man as he sat there in the safety of the Norman Manley International Airport. In Boston his relatives would be waiting for him to arrive and were all eager to meet his wife and children. He had decided not to return to Florida where he had lived for years before being forcibly returned to Jamaica, having been accused of petty larceny at the time. Back then his name was Livingston Johnson, spinster. On this day of his departure his name was Jonathan Livingston, Married with children. The plane arrived and the family boarded, and then just like that they were gone, from the horrors of living below the poverty line and having to do whatever is necessary to get by; from the ardent desire to fight against crime and criminality but realizing that . As the plane lifted away from the Airport Long John covered his face with his palms and sobbed quietly.

In Chudleigh Millicent got her good news one day when her uncle, Bertie called her and informed her that her Filing had been completed and she should start making plans to leave with him whenever he brought her Passport and Visa to her. He arrived and took her away as promised. Now Millicent lives in the United States with her father and his other family. Back in Jamaica the illiterate among those who succumb to pressure and entered the thug lifestyle, continues to succumb to its sucking confusing tentacles, but they never seem to learn. 'Blacks' who had rendered her a single parent had been shot and killed at the very lookout spot where they hung out with her dead baby daddy John Paul, leaving his girlfriend pregnant to become a single parent herself.

The thugs and their anonymous bosses never did discover who dismantled their operations, or even why they did it, and they probably never will.

Later that Tuesday evening after Jonathan Livingston and his family arrived in Boston, he made a telephone call back to Jamaica.

'Top Cop!" he shouted into the phone, *"Guess whey mi dey a chat to yu right now?!"*

"Whey yu dey, MoBay?!"

"As mi a chat to yu right now mi stan' up outside di Ohare International Airport inna Chicago Top Cop, a dey so di ting dey!" *"Mi tiad right now so afta mi get a likkle res'lata mi buzz yu back!"*

"A whey di raas yu a sey to mi?!"... "Bway Long John

yu switch up pon wi big time, an secretive wid it, but mi

happy fi yu nonetheless pawdi, congratulations an

maximum respec' fi da las' tip dey, it turn out really nice

an dem even promote the whole crew a'ready, anyway,

lata, as yu sey!"

Both phones hung up.

The End

Twisted Joke

By Sez Hoo

Downtown Manhattan. Monday morning, following a mugging two days earlier outside one of the many Barbershops along the street, my Jackass faced friend who just recently found a Glock pistol in the garbage near his home, the same 'Jackass face' who has never done an evil deed to another human being in his life, went into one of the Barbershops and sat in a chair.

The Barber approached him to do his hair. When the Barber opened his razor to start shaving, 'Jackass face' whipped out the empty 9mm Glock pistol and stuck it under his chin, as he reflected on the old Clint Eastwood movie in which the Western Star did a similar thing while being shaved.

"Be careful" he feigned a mean snarl at the Barber,
"I am a very bad man"

Right at that moment 'Jackass face' glanced out the
window and observed two uniformed Policemen
walking by.

Not wanting to take a joke too far and to risk going
to Prison, 'Jackass face' rammed the weapon into his
waistband, discharging a slug in the process which
hit him in his ankle. Writhing in agony, he raised
himself up, trying to laugh but with the pain
superseding he managed only a high-pitched wail.
'Jackass face' hobbled as quickly as he could, out the
door, past the two officers who had not heard the
discharge of the gun. They didn't even notice him;
caught up as they were in their morning chatter.

Suppressing the need to scream bloody murder and bring unwanted attention to himself, 'Jackass face' hopped and jumped on down the street on his good leg, as he tried to get to the nearest Hospital.

<u>The End</u>

Made in the USA
Monee, IL
23 December 2020